Cycles of Balance

Cycles of Balance

BOOK 2 OF THE MOON CYCLE TRILOGY

J.R. Shepherd

Contents

Epilogue

Special Thanks

Elimikoart on instagram for the cover art.
did a fantastic job

Steven Malloy Fine Art for all his contributions,
both on this book and the previous one

Everyone who helped me with editing and continuity
and who just enjoyed reading my stories

This book would have been much harder to finish without everyone
who helped me work on it.

My sincere thanks goes out to all of you.

Galbrea

Galbrea
Serriana
Gentry
Sea of Alenon
Telatia
Tyr' Anon
Serpent's Tongue
Port City
Hortaal
Laytrow
Val' Tora
Moon Witch Forest
Terramine
Mercury Mountains

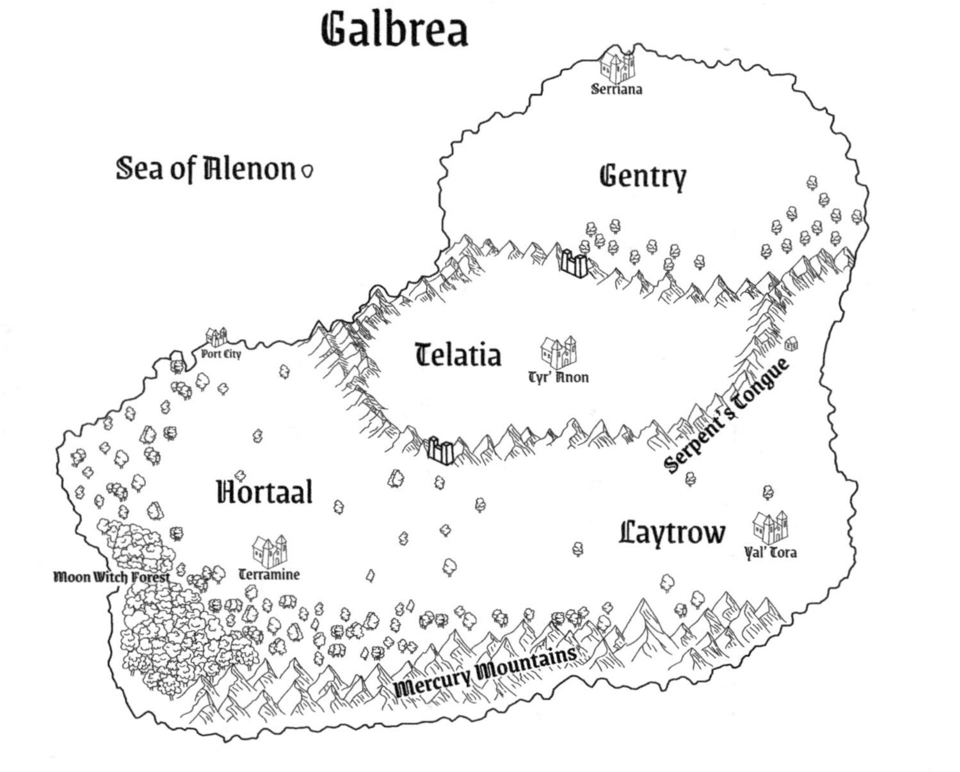

Prologue

"Come closer. Tiasia, that was your name was it not?" The girl nodded and went to stand just in front of where Rielle was sitting. She had short black hair that was mussed and dirty with leaves and sticks. She had brown eyes and, though she had dirt smudged on her face, freckles could be seen dotting her cheeks and nose. She wore a dappled brown cloak, a tattered little tunic, and a pair of simple breeches. Rielle looked over her for several moments. "She is the one." She stated matter-of-factly. The Matriarch looked back and forth between Rielle and Tiasia, struggling inwardly with the decision. "You will take care of her?" Rielle nodded. "Of course. No harm will come to her if I can prevent it."

"So your name is Rielle?" Tiasia asked as they rode the elevator to the forest floor where Rielle's horse waited patiently. Rielle nodded her head. "That's right." Tiasia fiddled with her hands. "And it was you who made that light that killed the weird looking monsters?" Rielle glanced down at the little girl. "So you were watching? Yes, I used magic to drive the monsters away." "And we will be fighting those things?" Tiasia immediately asked. Rielle paused for several seconds. "Yes, and it will be dangerous, so I want to make sure you understand that I need you to do everything I tell you, when I tell you to do it. I don't want anything to happen to you." Tiasia shrugged. "I can handle it."

Tiasia woke to a voice speaking quietly near the fire. She sat up and saw Rielle in a chair, with her back to the fire, seemingly talking to no one. "Who are you talking to?" Tiasia asked. Rielle hurriedly looked behind her at the little girl. "I am sorry, did I wake you?" Tiasia shook her head. "Not really. Who were you talking to?" Rielle's eyes trailed away for a moment and then she stood. "I think it is time that you met Master Solidus."

Vesth felt a tug at his sleeve and looked down to see the small girl standing beside him. She held out her hand and spoke. "I am Tiasia, nice to meet you." Vesth hesitated for a moment before taking the girl's small hand in a handshake. "I am Vesth, I am glad to meet your acquaintance as well." Tiasia looked at Rielle. "Oooh, he is very proper isn't he?" Vesth gave the girl a strange look and Rielle laughed.

Rielle and Tiasia giggled and laughed until Rielle gained enough control to speak again. "Sir Segine, have you ever done something simply for the fun of it?" The big knight gave her a strange look. "I am not sure I understand what you mean." Tiasia scoffed. "A game, you silly. Have you ever played a game?" The little girl looked at both men. Segine shrugged. "When I was very young perhaps." Tiasia and Rielle looked at Vesth. Vesth shifted uncomfortably. "I have never understood the need to play games before. I do not see any benefit to be gained from it." Rielle stared in surprise. Tiasia's eyes widened. "You have never played a single game before?" Vesth shook his head and Tiasia's eyes widened further. "That is sad. We have to play, right now." Without waiting for permission, Tiasia grabbed

Segine's hand and dragged him towards the door. Unsure of what else to do, the knight followed her without trouble.

"Tiasia." The little girl peaked out from behind Vesth and looked at Rielle. "Yes?" She asked timidly. Rielle motioned to her and she quickly ran to her side. "Tiasia, this is our new friend, Nysisset. Hold her hand and have her show you how we can get back to Master Solidus's home." Tiasia nodded and ran to Nysisset's side and took hold of one of her hands. Nysisset looked down at the little girl with a dumbfounded expression. "Come on miss Nysisset, lets go." Tiasia said and dragged Nysisset off, back through the room full of gold. Nysisset quickly recovered and tried to remove the little girl from her hand, but could not, no matter what she tried.

They stood silently for a moment and then Nysisset turned when she heard a giggle. Vesth had lifted Tiasia up into her saddle and the little girl was laughing and hugging her horse around it's neck and playing with it's mane and ears. The horse accepted everything patiently and even seemed to enjoy the attention given by the little girl.

"Maybe you would feel better sitting outside." Tiasia suggested, wiping her soapy hands on the front of her tunic. "Don't you have someone else to bother?" Nysisset asked moodily. Tiasia grinned. "Sure, but they aren't as much fun to talk to." Nysisset sighed. "Why don't you go steal something then?" Tiasia traced a circle on the ground with her foot. "Stealing is wrong, and miss Rielle already slapped my wrist for sticking a spoon in my pocket after I had washed it." Nysisset felt herself smile at this. She made sure she had a straight face and then stood and made her way towards the door. "Maybe I should go outside." She said. Tiasia grinned happily at her as she went and then turned and went back into the kitchen.

Nysisset shook her head. "I don't know why that girl gets to me." She said as she closed the door behind her. Tiasia peaked around the corner at the door. "It's because I'm sneaky and so darn cute."

"Tiasia. She is gone." She cried. Nysisset stood awkwardly for a moment and then wrapped her arms around Rielle. "I know. But I will guide her to the heaven realm where she can be safe and happy." The events from previous days floated back to Rielle with painful clarity as she sat quietly in the room she had been given. A knock sounded in the room and the door opened. Vesth took a step in and looked around before spotting Rielle. He watched her quietly for a few moments and then motioned with his hand. "Come with me, you need to do something to keep your mind clear." Rielle shook her head and stared at the floor. Vesth sighed and fully entered the room, making his way to Rielle's side and taking hold of her hand. "Come." He repeated and lifted her to her feet. Rielle hung her head and followed him without further struggle.

1

Chapter one

Rielle swiped at Vesth with her wooden practice sword, stumbling forward as Vesth sidestepped the attack. She recovered as quickly as she could and turned to block Vesth's attack. Their swords met for a moment and then Rielle pushed Vesth away and swung again.

Vesth had forced her to practice her sword forms and then spar with him. They had been at it for a few hours and Rielle realized that he had done so to keep her mind occupied. Vesth noticed her sudden loss of concentration and gave her a sharp rap against one shoulder to bring her attention back. Rielle rolled her shoulder to try and make the stinging stop and then lunged at Vesth.

Eventually Rielle collapsed, too tired to continue.

"I can't keep this up." She panted. Vesth nodded and made a short bow before returning his wooden sword to a rack against one end of the room they had been using for practice.

"I am surprised you lasted as long as you did." Said a voice from the doorway. Vesth turned to see Marina leaning against the door frame.

"Lady Marina." Vesth bowed. "I hope we have not been disturbing anyone." Marina shook her head.

"Not at all. I am glad to see you doing something besides sulking." Vesth nodded.

"I cannot afford to let myself." Marina smiled kindly.

"Of course, and I am glad you got Rielle back onto her feet. Though, I am surprised at how long she was able to fight. Only a few days ago she was completely drained of strength." Rielle struggled to her feet.

"I am fine." She said, wobbling a little as she made her slow way toward the sword rack. Vesth stepped to her side and gently took the sword from her hands and placed one hand under her arm for support.

"Thank you." She said quietly. Vesth nodded but said nothing. Vesth lead Rielle to a bench and let her sit before returning her sword to its proper place.

"I think I will search out Segine for a while, If you think you will be alright here on your own." He told Rielle. She nodded carefully.

"I will be fine." Vesth half bowed to her and then to Marina before heading out the door.

"I believe he was last seen outside the main doors, hacking at bundles of grass, if you are interested." Marina told him. Vesth nodded and muttered a thank you and disappeared. Marina watched him go and then sat down beside Rielle, waiting silently for several minutes before she spoke.

"Have you heard from Solidus yet?" She asked Rielle. Rielle

stared at the floor. "No, not yet." Marina sadly stared at the far wall.

"He is being very hard on himself. He always has been when he has to watch something come to pass and not being able to act to prevent it." A tear rolled down Rielle's face. Marina looked to her own feet.

"I am sorry. I shouldn't be dredging up fresh wounds so close to when they were inflicted." Rielle nodded and wiped the tears from her eyes.

"It's ok. I know that Solidus would have done something if he could. I could feel his pain, before he destroyed that demon and then disappeared. But why must he endure so much? And why did she have to die after so little time with us? Wasn't she supposed to be an important part of restoring balance to the world?" Marina nodded slowly.

" 'A strong life force is heaven bade. a being both fear and angel as one. These strong souls to heal what's been done. The one that the angel helps transcend, in aid to another as the trials near their end.' It is not entirely clear what will happen, only Solidus can see that, but from the passages in the prediction it seems like Tiasia had something important to do. Something she could only accomplish in the Heaven Realm. What that could be is beyond my comprehension." Rielle looked up at Marina. The woman was as young in appearance as Solidus had been and her silver hair reached her waist. Her eyes were a beautiful clear blue and her face was only marred by a few streaks of ash.

"It seems so strange that you and Solidus both look so young and vibrant, and Agamemnon seems to be an old man." Marina smiled, glad to change the subject.

"It is our balance. Two of us remain in bodies that are forever young, and the other two, though never aging, live in older bodies. Agamemnon chose to appear older, as he felt a temple high priest should seem old and wise. Solidus chose to seem young because it would be easier for him to wander the world unnoticed. We couldn't decide who should be the young one between myself and Delgorin, so we flipped a coin and I won the opportunity to be young."

"Delgorin?" Rielle asked. Marina laughed.

"Oh, that is right, I don't suppose Solidus told you about the rest of us." Rielle shook her head. "Not really, he just told us that we would meet him when the time came." Marina nodded her head. "And you shall. Travel Mage Gartiel Delgorin is the third of the four Alenon Mages. He is sneaky and childish and, even though he looks like a wizened old stump, he is a very smooth talker. He could probably sell someone a handful of dirt for a half dozen gold pieces if he set his mind to it. But despite his childish ways, and his ability to sell almost anything, he is one of the greatest masters of traveling magic to ever wander Galbrea and the lands beyond." Rielle nodded and thought for a moment.

"It seems to me that every one of the Alenon Mages is the greatest mage to ever come along in one way or another." Marina chuckled.

"It does seem that way doesn't it? For starters, Alenon was a kingdom of skilled magic users. The other kingdoms had their mages, but the mages of Alenon were extremely gifted and revered for their power. But those few who reach their full potential gain a certain, presence of mind. The four of us who remain were such, which is why our Deity chose us to be her closest servants. We did as she directed us and we knew that the world was in balance for the strength of the Six Deities. Because of this, we were protected when Alenon was destroyed." A hint of sadness washed over Marina for a moment before she continued.

"However, Agamemnon is actually the only one of us who has no peer. Even Solidus is not the greatest mage to ever have lived, though he is not far off. But being the best also has its weaknesses. Agamemnon is the greatest Shield Mage to ever live, but his combat skills are virtually zero. And Solidus or myself could break through his barriers, given the time and the use of a little effort. Delgorin is not the most powerful, but he is very good at what he does. He is a master of traveling magic. Magic that could transport him a few feet, or halfway across the world in an instant. He is also a skilled fighter and a decent shield mage, but again, he is not a match for someone gifted in combat. Solidus, on the other hand, is a balance mage, one of the most gifted ever born. There were only two before him who were more powerful and their names were all but lost to the ages, known only to Solidus and our Deity. Even I am only barely old enough to remember them, and I never learned their names. The difference between a specifically skilled mage and a balance mage is that a balance mage is essentially gifted in all types of magic. Any spell that any of the rest of us could cast, Solidus can match. He could easily over power any one of us, he is also capable of creating barriers almost as powerful as Agamemnon's. However, Solidus may also have the single greatest weakness out of all of us. As a Balance Mage, Solidus is bound by a thousand times more rules than a normal mage. Where a normal mage can simply call fire to his hand and use it on something, Solidus must cool something else in equal parts to allow him to conjure that same fire. He is also the only remaining balance mage left to this world, and so it is his duty to watch all predictions and do what he can to keep the world in balance. Some things he must simply let happen, however much it tears him apart to do so." Rielle suddenly began to understand why Solidus was the way he was. Marina continued.

"And sometimes he must do things to maintain balance that he would prefer he didn't have to do. A long time ago, the Chaos Order tried to unbalance the world and Solidus was forced to destroy nearly all life in Telatia to bring everything back into balance. He pushed the world to the brink, and nearly unbalanced it himself and, in so doing, he caused Telatia to become the wasteland that it is." Rielle looked at Marina, not entirely comprehending. Marina saddened.

"Solidus is the reason why Telatia is a desert. It was once a lush, tropical land, filled with springs and oasis' that caused life to bloom in nearly every corner. But when Solidus destroyed the demons that had overrun Tyr' Anon, the water ceased to flow, the plant life withered and died, and many of the fairies and spirits that dwelled there were warped and twisted in anguish over the loss of their fertile home. It is Solidus's single greatest regret in a four thousand year long list of regrets." Rielle felt another tear come to her eye, this time for Solidus. She sniffled and hurriedly changed the subject.

"And what kind of mage are you?" Marina seemed a little surprised before she put on a smile. "Ah yes, what could there be left for me after everything else, right?" Rielle glanced away with a nod, her cheeks turning pink. Marina's smile grew.

"My brothers are all very grand and powerful. Each, besides Solidus, with very specific powers in which they are gifted. I, However, am a little different. I am skilled in both defensive and offensive magic, as well as a steady hand with all manner of physical weapons. I am what is called, a Battle Mage. In Alenon, those born with the gift to become Battle Mages are almost as rare as those born to become Balance Mages." Marina paused for a moment and stared at Rielle.

"And now that you mention it, what color of magic flows through you?" Rielle looked at Marina questioningly.

"I am not sure what you mean." Marina nodded with an apologetic smile.

"Of course, I am sorry. I often forget that the time of magic has passed and that the knowledge of magic is not common anymore. When magic was still widely practiced, and a person was found to have magical talent, they were given a test to see what the color of their inner power was. Through that, it could be determined what kind of magic the person would be skilled in. The basic, and most common magics, were easy to identify. Red, blue, green, or grey energy was the sign that one was skilled in one of the four elements. Yellow signified the power to travel through magic. And white magic showed that one could raise powerful shields and perform healing magic." Rielle nodded her understanding. "And what about Silver? Solidus's magic is silver, what does that show?" Marina shrugged.

"To be honest, no one is entirely sure. Solidus is the only one in known history born with silver magic. It may signify a gift in all types of magic, or a type of magic we have never seen before. Only Solidus himself truly knows that secret, and he would never speak of it. However, that is beside the point.

Before you were taught, you would have been given a test to see the color of your power. But with Solidus as your teacher, I am sure he could already see the color of your power before he even mentioned magic to you. He probably didn't even say anything and just went straight to teaching you. What has he taught you so far?" Rielle rubbed her nose in thought.

"He first taught me to raise and lower a shield, then he taught me to form a ball of light, and, most recently, he taught me how to create and repel fire." Marina nodded. "Almost all defensive magic, perhaps you are a shield mage like Agamemnon, we shall see." Marina stood and motioned for Rielle to do the same.

"I think it is time we give you a proper test." Rielle nodded and stood, a little shakily. Marina smiled.

"I know you are tired, but this will take very little strength to accomplish." Rielle nodded her readiness. Marina held her arms out in front of her and Rielle did the same. "Will your power to beat faster, enough so you can feel it pulse all the way through you. Then hold your hands close together and create the space you would use to make a spell of light, but do not fill it with light." Rielle did as she was told and soon there was a small rippling patch of air between her hands. Marina nodded.

"Now just let your power flow between your hands, up through one arm and down the other. Don't force it, just let it happen." Rielle nodded and tried to imagine that her power could flow in a circle. As she watched, a faint pulse of light beat between her hands, as if she were watching a blood vein close to the skin, throbbing with blood. "Good." Marina told her. "Now let your power build and grow so that the light can get brighter." Rielle nodded and willed her inner power to beat faster. The pulsing light between her hands grew until a brilliant purple bolt of lightning flashed between her hands in time to the beating of her inner power. Marina nodded.

"You may slow your power and sit again if you wish." Rielle slowed her inner power and the light between her hands faded away. She felt a little drained and carefully lowered herself back onto the bench.

"I see now what Solidus saw in you." Marina said, an excited smile on her face. "Your inner power is purple, you are like me. You have been gifted as a Battle Mage."

* * *

Rielle stood across from Marina, her hands set in a stance Marina had taught her. Marina watched carefully, her own hands a mirror image of Rielle's. They circled for several moments before Marina made a quick step forward and a small gesture, causing a fiery projectile to shoot from her finger tips. Rielle sidestepped and batted the attack aside with her fingers, then countered with a similar projectile. Marina captured the projectile between her hands and forced it to fade away.

"Very good. You are catching on quickly, and after only a couple days of practice at that." Rielle relaxed and half bowed.

"Thank you, Mistress Marina, you are an excellent teacher."

"*Even better than I am?*" The voice echoed inside Rielle's head. Rielle gasped in surprise and straightened.

"*Master Solidus, You are back!*" Rielle felt Solidus nod.

"*Indeed I am. I have had sufficient time to rest and... other things. Now we need to be moving. There is something that must be seen to.*"

"Are you well Rielle?" Marina asked. Rielle jumped slightly and smiled.

"Of course."

"May I speak with Marina for a moment?" Solidus asked.

"Of course." Rielle repeated aloud. Her breath came in short gasps for a moment as the familiar feel of Solidus taking control of her body filled her senses. Marina stared for a moment in surprise and then smiled.

"Hello brother." She stated simply. Rielle felt herself smile.

"Hello little sister. I thank you for teaching Rielle in my absence." Marina folded her arms across her chest.

"Well someone had to, didn't they? I am rather surprised you took so long to recover." Rielle/Solidus shrugged.

"I was taxed. And I had other things to occupy my mind. And some things which must be investigated now that I am recovered completely." Marina nodded.

"I see. How do you plan to proceed?" Rielle/Solidus looked to the sky.

"For now, I must attend to Borsa. He has done something very foolish that must be fixed, if at all possible. If not... I may have to do something foolish myself." Marina watched Solidus carefully.

"Solidus, I hope you do not mean to do what I think you do." Solidus looked back at Marina.

"Only if necessary. Until then, there is a matter of your charge. Are you prepared?" Marina let her arms fall to her sides.

"I am, mostly. The seals are all I have left to engrave, then it will be complete. your initial seals have held well enough these past years that I have been putting off creating new ones." Rielle/Solidus nodded.

"Good, We will need it by tonight, I wish to leave in the morning at sunrise." Marina nodded.

"Yes, Solidus. It will be ready." Rielle/Solidus smiled. "I am pleased to see you again after so long Marina." Marina smiled again.

"And I you. Though you take a different form, you are still the same Solidus." Rielle/Solidus nodded.

"I am too old to change now. But even I still have a few tricks left up my sleeves. For now I will let Rielle have her body back. She can gather the others together and inform them on what they are to do." Marina smiled and half bowed.

"Be well brother." Rielle/Solidus returned the gesture.

"And you, little sister." Rielle's eyes returned to normal as she straightened back up.

"So it is time to leave already then." She said, a little sadly. Marina smiled.

"You will be back before you know it. But right now you have other duties to perform. And the High Priest Borsa will only become more powerful with time." Rielle nodded.

"Yes. I think I will go and do as Solidus instructed and seek out the others." Marina nodded.

"I will meet you at the temple doors in the morning to see you off." Rielle smiled at the mage and then turned and left the room.

"Be careful." Marina said quietly after Rielle had left. "And you," She stated more loudly, without turning.

"You may come out of hiding." There was a moment's pause and then Nysisset stepped out from a dark corner.

"So we are leaving then. Finally I can pay Borsa back for the trouble he has caused me." Marina turned and looked at the young woman.

"Be very careful to keep hold of your emotion, young one.

Borsa is not to be trifled with, even Solidus is being careful with this. You must not stray from your path." Nysisset scowled.

"What do I care about my path. Even I am not so callous as to negligently kill without thought." Marina nodded, a smile half creeping onto her face.

"But that is exactly what you plan for Borsa." Nysisset opened her mouth to deny it, but Marina held up a hand to silence her.

"You would let your emotions loose and simply attack the High Priest. But think carefully about what you are planning. Even Solidus, as powerful as he is, chose not to fight Borsa when he first spoke with him. He chose instead to try and talk him out of his chosen path. How much more powerful will Borsa be now that he has taken a Demon inside his body? And you still think that you are any match for him?" Nysisset glared moodily at the ground. Marina nodded.

"Do you understand now? I know it is your way to take back what has been taken from you, and you will get your revenge in time, But you must listen and do as Solidus tells you. Remember, he knows how you feel and feels much the same. He also already knows what is going to happen. Let him guide you. Follow him and he will show you where to go." Nysisset sighed.

"Fine. But I won't pass up another chance if I get it." Marina smiled.

"Of course you won't. Now, you should meet with Rielle and the other two. I am sure you will want to be able to put in your own opinion about how to proceed." Nysisset nodded sharply and left the room at a fast pace. Marina shook her head as she left. "Strong willed child."

2

Chapter two

"Are you sure we have time to sit and wait? Daylight is burning and we have a long way to go." Nysisset said, agitation clear in her voice. Rielle simply watched the door to the temple.

"We do not have as far to go as you might think. Besides, Solidus says that Marina has something we need and we must get it before we leave. There might not be time afterwards." Nysisset sighed heavily and slumped in her saddle.

They sat quietly for several minutes, the horses standing nervously, waiting to leave. Finally the doors to the temple swung open and Marina stepped out into the morning sunlight. She was holding a long, tightly rolled cloth tied with several silken ropes.

"Please forgive my lateness." She called to them. "It took me longer to finish than I expected."

"Oh don't mind us." Nysisset said loudly. "We are only on a quest to save the whole world from total destruction, so there is no need to hurry." Marina smiled happily. "I see you are in a fine mood today Nysisset." Nysisset grumbled but didn't answer.

"Anyway, now that I am finished you may be on your way." Marina held out the rolled cloth out at arm's length and Rielle accepted it with a nod.

"Thank you, I am sure it wasn't easy to finish." Marina laughed lightly.

"Oh think nothing of it. I have been working on that for nearly eight hundred years. It had to get finished at some point."

"Eight hundred years?" Segine sputtered. "It took that long to make...er, whatever it is?" Marina smiled at the knight.

"I worked off and on. I guess if I had worked straight through it would only have taken me a hundred or so years to complete."

"But what is it?" Vesth asked. Marina smiled innocently.

"That remains to be seen. You will just have to wait until Rielle is ready, or Solidus sees fit to use it." Segine scowled but Vesth just shrugged and left it at that. Rielle finished tying the cloth across her back and adjusted it so it was comfortable.

"We will be off then. Thank you for your help Marina." Marina nodded and then the smile drifted away from her face.

"Just be very careful, Tiamat does not like to be disturbed." Rielle nodded.

"Of course, we will." With this, Rielle bowed in her saddle and then turned her horse and headed down the mountain the way they had come on the night of the Blood Moon Cycle. The others, each in turn, bowed to Marina and then turned to follow Rielle. Several minutes went by as they steadily rode before Nysisset finally spoke again. "Are we really going to go through Lord Tiamat's territory?" Rielle nodded. "Both Great Gates have been destroyed. Tiamat's cave is the only viable way into Telatia now." Segine scratched his chin.

"Where have I heard that name before?" Rielle shuddered and Solidus took over and spoke.

"He is a legend passed down through Telatia. An enormous Fire Dragon, one of four ancient and powerful creatures, who helped the Six Deities forge the world."

"A dragon?" Segine asked in wonder.

"I don't like the sound of this." Vesth said. Rielle/Solidus nodded.

"After the world was complete the four creatures, including Tiamat, sealed themselves away to keep an eye over the elements and ensure that no single element would tip the balance on its own." Segine nodded.

"This Tiamat doesn't seem like such a bad guy." Solidus scoffed.

"He is short tempered and intolerant of humans. It would be best if we do not wake him on our way through his caverns."

"And if he does wake up, then what?" Vesth asked. Nysisset shivered.

"The haunted wastes of Telatia are filled with spirits and sprites and fairies. Each warped and twisted in agony over the loss of their once fertile home. The shrieks and howls and screams, not to mention the mirages and illusions, are enough to drive even the most devout and religious knight to insanity." Rielle nodded and Solidus spoke.

"But even that cursed place falls still when Tiamat stirs."

* * *

The scent of brimstone, as well as decay, wafted strongly from the slim cave entrance.

"Are you sure this is the place? It looks like a crack that leads straight into the void to me." Segine eyed the narrow passage suspiciously. "I don't see how you plan to get the horses in there." Nysisset said testily. Rielle nodded.

"Yes, this is the place. And we won't be taking the horses with us. Their presence would only increase the chance of Tiamat waking while we are here. We will go on foot." Vesth shook his head.

"I don't like this." Rielle half smiled without emotion.

"You don't need to like it Vesth. This is the only way open to us for now." Vesth grimaced, but nodded and dismounted. The others followed his example and stood, waiting quietly. Rielle turned and patted her horse's neck before releasing its reigns and pushing it slightly to turn it away from the cave and back down the path they had followed. Then she turned back and started towards the cave.

"What of the horses?" Segine asked. Rielle waved without looking back.

"They will find us again when we need them." Then she disappeared into the dark crevice in the rock. Nysisset shrugged and released her horse before quickly following Rielle into the dark. Segine looked to Vesth for help. Vesth shook his head.

"I don't like this." He repeated, then he let go of the reigns and followed where the others had gone. Segine struggled inwardly with himself for a few moments before looking at his charger apologetically and rushing to catch up with the others.

The way was cramped and the air stuffy. Moist, hot air

seemed to flow from the depths of the cavern and a pale fungus glowed faintly, providing them with enough light to navigate their way. The walls were nearly smooth, as if they had been carved by unknown hands and polished until there were no visible flaws.

"Is this cave natural?" Segine asked, brushing one wall with his fingers. The fungus smeared and left a trace of light on his fingertips.

"As natural as the mountains they travel through." Rielle stated. "And be careful not to get any of the fungus in your eyes, you will go blind." Segine looked at his fingers in horror and quickly tried to wipe them off on his armor, leaving little fading trails of light.

"Don't be such a wimp." Nysisset growled as she glanced over her shoulder. Segine harrumphed, but grudgingly let his hand drop to his side. They walked for several minutes before Rielle called a halt. They stood quietly for a moment and then Rielle turned around, her eyes a brilliant silver that glowed along with the light around them. "From here on you must be very careful." Solidus spoke quietly. "We do not want lord Tiamat to wake before we reach the other side. Do not speak, no matter what happens." Solidus watched for a moment to make sure they all understood, and then turned and led them around a bend.

Once they rounded the corner, it seemed as if they had entered the pits of the underworld itself. Great cracks and fissures covered the floor, angry red light emanating from them. A dull humming could be heard reverberating around the cavernous room they had entered. In places, spatters of red hot liquid could be seen spraying out of a few of the largest cracks.

At the far end of the room, just at the edge of their vision, they could see a small opening like the one through which they had entered. Rielle set off across the fiery landscape and the others followed, weaving in and out of the cracks, avoiding the ones spewing the liquid out onto the floor. Segine was certain they were going to make it after they had crossed more than half way, but they were halted in their tracks.

"You didn't honestly think you were going to get through here under my notice did you?" The voice hissed out of the darkness and caused all those it fell upon to shake. "You should know better, Master Solidus." Solidus sighed and Rielle turned, motioning for the others to get behind her.

"I simply did not wish to disturb your sleep, Lord Tiamat. I know how much you detest being woken." A loud rumble filled the air and the entire cavern wall seemed to rise and move. If Rielle had been in control of her own body, she probably would have collapsed. The dragon before them was easily three hundred feet long and towered over them as if they were nothing more than ants at his feet.

"You are correct, Silver Mage, I do not like to be awakened from my slumber. But what brings you to the conclusion that recent events would not already have brought me out of the world of dreams?" Solidus nodded.

"Of course, forgive me for my assumption. I, unfortunately, had very little control of the outcome of recent events. Had I been able to do more, perhaps you would not have woken." The dragon craned his neck and turned to face Solidus. His eyes opened and it was as if one had opened the doors to a furnace. Brilliant red and yellow light poured from them and radiated heat almost to the point of flames.

"Perhaps." The dragon grumbled. "Leviathan is also not pleased with what you have done. Our elements were troubled for some time after the fact. You have broken a very strict law Solidus, and I don't think you will soon recover from it." Solidus nodded sadly.

"Indeed, I have broken the law in causing a creature to cease its existence, But I assure you I have already paid heavily for that infraction. I am also sure that I will continue to pay for some time, but for now I have other things to attend to. I am sure you know what goes on beyond your own mountains." A low menacing rumble filled the air. "That fool has further tainted my grounds. Should he cross my path he will burn eternally." Solidus nodded.

"I am sure Borsa is not so foolish as to cross you, Lord Tiamat. He is likely to stay holed up in his temple unless he is driven out."

"And you intend to do this?" The dragon asked. Solidus nodded.

"If I can. If not, other pieces will be set into motion and I do not think you will be able to sleep much longer." The dragon growled again.

"You have not the power, in your current mortal form. I should devour you all now and deal with Borsa myself." Stones and dust rose from the ground as power rippled and flowed from Solidus.

"Do not seek to bar my path, Tiamat. This is the prediction and it will be fulfilled. The Balance will not shift, and I think you will find that I wield plenty of power even from within this mortal girl." For a moment, Rielle was angry at being called 'mortal girl'. But that anger was quickly replaced by fear as Tiamat rose up on all four legs and pulled back his head, as if to strike.

The dragon's mouth opened and molten flame poured from deep within him and crossed the cavern in a roaring tide. Solidus stood his ground, and a silver barrier surrounded everyone. The flames flowed smoothly across the barrier and Rielle felt tremendous pressure across her entire body. After what seemed like an eternity, the flames ceased and the roaring died away. Tiamat glared dangerously down at them and Solidus glared back, power racing through his silver eyes. After several moments, Tiamat finally laid down again.

"Go, leave my sanctuary. Quickly, before I change my mind. I will not be so kind if you wake me a second time." Solidus bowed.

"As you wish, Lord Tiamat." Rielle turned and Shepherded the others through the narrow passage and away from the overwhelming presence of the dragon.

"Borsa's ambition has caused the spirits to stir, Master Solidus." Rielle nodded and Solidus spoke, even as the others were being pushed along.

"Of this I am aware, Lord Tiamat. And I am already prepared to take precautions. I am also hoping that, with your recent awakening, the spirits will stay hidden a while longer." The Dragon grumbled as he wrapped his long neck around his body to sleep once more.

"I would not count on it." Rielle propelled the others through the small opening and into another narrow passageway. They hurried on, the thoughts of what lay behind driving them forward. It was not long before they saw a thin crack of light before them and they left the cave.

They all heaved a sigh of relief and Segine slumped against the jagged rock of the mountains. Rielle took a few more steps and looked out over the landscape. Heat radiated over the sand in liquid waves as far as the eye could see. The air was still, but it seemed as if it could change at any moment. Rielle breathed deeply through her nose.

"We will have to be very careful. The spirits are waking." Vesth joined Rielle and looked out over the desert.

"What spirits?"

"The twisted spirits of those who lost their fertile land over fifteen hundred years ago." Nysisset answered.

"We stand very little chance of making it to Tyr' Anon before they find us." Vesth continued to stare stoically into space.

"What happens if they do find us?" Rielle shuddered involuntarily.

"Human minds were not meant to experience such grief and pain. We would be driven insane, at the very least, and it would very likely kill us." Nysisset nodded her agreement.

"Even I would not last long." She admitted.

"You aren't human?" Segine asked, gathering himself enough to push away from the mountain side and stand on his own.

"I don't suppose it should surprise you. I mentioned once before I am a shape shifter." Nysisset said smugly. "I am a personal servant of the Deity of Evil. He would not pick something so weak as a human to serve him."

"And yet, the human form is the one most often taken by a Deity who wishes to appear to others." Rielle stated, a smile creeping onto her face as she looked back at Nysisset.

"The humans are much greater than you give them credit for." Nysisset scowled but shrugged.

"I am unconvinced. I am, however, curious as to how you plan to get us across the desert alive." Rielle looked back out over the sand.

"The same way Solidus took me across when he destroyed the Great Gates. I will put all of us into an enchanted sleep and Solidus will guide us to Tyr' Anon." Segine scowled.

"I don't think that is a good idea. How can we fight if we are asleep?" Vesth nodded.

"I agree with Segine. How can we defend ourselves if we are asleep? And how will we even walk for that matter?" Rielle sighed.

"Think of it as sleep walking. Part of your mind remains aware when you are asleep. Solidus will control that part of you and have you walk beside him. As for defending yourselves, The idea is to make sure we don't have to. If we get into any real danger, Solidus will wake you so that you may fight. However, there is not much left in the wastes of Telatia that can cause us any physical threat. Your mind is more at risk here than your body." Vesth nodded.

"Very well. If that is what must be done." Segine shook his head.

"I still don't like it. Sneaking around doesn't seem very honorable."

"And how, exactly, is dying before you have a chance to fight any more honorable?" Nysisset asked. "The world is not an honorable place. It is best to throw honor out of your way and just make sure things get done." Segine shook his head again.

"It is thinking like that that makes my honor even more impor-tant." Nysisset folded her arms and stuck her nose in the air.

"That is enough of that." Vesth stated emphatically. "We have a task to perform and this is the only way to do it. I will not hear any arguments on the subject." Nysisset gave a slight nod and Segine followed suit. Rielle gave Vesth an appreciative look and then turned around to face everyone.

"This will be very quick and you will be waking up before you know it. It may be hours or days from now, but time is not the important thing. Everyone relax and let yourself sleep when the feeling comes." Vesth nodded and then eyed the other two. They both nodded, Segine somewhat grudgingly.

Rielle moved first to Segine. She stood quietly for a few moments, concentrating on Solidus's instruction, then waved one hand across Segine's face. She mumbled a few words and Segine's eyes fluttered and then fell closed. He slouched slightly, but remained standing. Rielle turned to Nysisset.

"Relax, Nysisset, the sooner you do, the sooner you will be where you want to be." Nysisset grumbled but let her arms fall to her sides and relaxed her body. Rielle did the same thing she did to Segine and Nysisset closed her eyes and, though she remained standing, her body went limp. Lastly Rielle turned to Vesth.

"Are you ready?" She asked him. Vesth nodded.

"As much as I ever will be." Rielle half smiled and waved her hands across his face. Vesth struggled to stay awake for a few seconds and then succumbed to the magical sleep. Rielle checked each of them and then nodded.

"*Are you ready to begin?*" Solidus asked her. Rielle nodded again.

"Yes, the faster we move, the better." She felt Solidus nod and then her eyes closed and her thoughts grew dim until she had completely fallen asleep. Solidus breathed deeply a few times and then made a simple movement towards each of the other three.

A small silver thread attached to each of them in the center of their chest and they each stood up straight, as if under their own power. Solidus turned and headed out across the sand, the others following obediently behind. Very quickly the wind began to pick up and Solidus could smell something in the air that made him quicken his pace.

"May our journey be a short one." He said aloud.

3

Chapter Three

Vesth's eyes fluttered open and blinked a few times, raising one hand to shield his eyes from the early morning light. Rielle moved to the others and brought her hand across their faces to wake them. Vesth looked around and found that they were standing before the front gate of an enormous city of black stone. He inspected it and frowned. "Something isn't right." He said aloud. The others looked at him, Segine rubbing the sleep from one eye.

"What do you mean?" Vesth shook his head.

"I don't know. Something about the city is wrong." Rielle looked back at the city gate.

"This city was tainted long ago by demons that were summoned here. That taint permeates everything here." Rielle saddened visibly. Vesth noticed immediately.

"What is wrong?" Rielle shook her head.

"We should go. The less time that we have to spend in this place, the better." They entered through a small door set inside the main gate and entered the city. Rielle followed the path they had when Solidus had first brought her to Tyr' Anon. They traveled carefully along the streets and up the first flight of stairs to the second tier.

"It is very quiet." Nysisset observed, looking around. Vesth's trained eyes scanned everything thoroughly.

"Where is everyone?" Segine glanced behind them over the first tier of the city. "The city is abandoned." He said. Rielle shook her head.

"No, Tyr' Anon was not abandoned." Segine moved ahead of the group and peered into the windows facing the street. Vesth joined him and they worked their way along each side of the street, peering into windows and doorways.

"It sure looks abandoned to me." Segine said after some time of searching. "There is nobody. No people, no animals, not even insects as far as I can tell." Rielle nodded sadly and pointed at a window.

"And yet, in many of these homes, cold meals sit uneaten. Work remains half done. Weapons lay discarded on the ground. Everything that you see speaks of life in this city, and yet there is no one here remaining to do these things. Everything is silent and still." A shudder ran through the ground around them and a sharp crack was heard from the direction of the temple.

"Apparently not everything." Nysisset said. Rielle nodded.

"We must hurry." They picked up the pace and moved onward and up the second flight of stairs to the third tier.

Another tremor shook the ground and another resounding crack filled the air as they neared the temple. They reached the bottom of the stairs to the temple and stopped. Rielle shook slightly and Solidus took control.

"Everyone be very careful from here. Do not, under any

circumstances, try to confront Borsa on your own. Leave him to me." Nysisset scowled, but they all nodded. Rielle nodded back and they made their way up to the temple, stepping over discarded spears as they went. Solidus opened the doors and stepped inside, the others following closely behind. Inside, the air was heavy and stale. Vesth felt that, with each drawn breath, he was being corrupted, poisoned by the very air in the temple.

"This taint is foul." Nysisset growled. Rielle simply nodded and motioned for them to continue following. Had Solidus not known the way, Vesth was certain they would have become hopelessly lost. The temple was a labyrinth of hallways and doors and arches and the layout made no structural sense. Branching halls and rooms lay in seemingly absurd directions and angles. Vesth shook his head and concentrated on following Rielle.

Minutes passed and finally they came to a large door covered in strange symbols that glowed with an eerie light. Rielle walked within arm's reach of the door and stopped. They waited for several seconds and Segine opened his mouth to ask what they were waiting for. Nysisset clamped a hand over his mouth and pointed as the doors swung inward, revealing a large room laying in disarray. Furniture was smashed, the floor was scorched, and a cracked altar lay in two pieces on the opposite end of the room.

"I had almost forgotten you had survived my previous aggression." Came a voice from within the room.

"I carry the scars with me still, Borsa." Rielle replied, carefully entering the room. The room echoed with a haunting chuckle and Borsa stood from where he had been sitting before the destroyed altar.

"I hope you can forgive my lack of control then. It does not befit a priest to let his emotions rule him." Rielle stopped just inside the door.

"That is in the past now. Since then you have done much more destructive and evil things. For those, there is no forgiveness." The chuckle returned.

"Student of Solidus, you are." Borsa turned and it took all of Rielle's will not to turn away in disgust. Borsa had become tainted from his contact with the power of the chaos. Streaks of dead, black flesh marbled his skin. Cracks in his skin oozed yellow puss that bubbled and hissed. And on top of that his features were still as handsome as they had been when Rielle had first seen him, though more sickly and gaunt. Rielle resisted the urge to scream and, instead, spoke calmly.

"Look at what you have done, even to yourself Borsa. You have destroyed what made you human." Borsa smiled, his skin stretching tight and forcing more puss to ooze from the cracks.

"Why would I want to be human? I have more power now than anyone has ever dreamed. Why would I wish to go back to my weak and helpless humanity?" Nysisset snarled and Vesth placed a restraining hand on her arm. Borsa glanced behind Rielle, seemingly noticing the others for the first time.

"Have you brought these with you to help you fight me?" Rielle looked behind her and then back to Borsa.

"No, they are of no consequence to you. I am who you will face." Borsa's smile widened.

"You seem very confident in yourself. Did Solidus really teach you so much before he passed?" Rielle half smiled.

"Of course not, but he has taught me a great deal since." The smiled faded away from the priest's face.

"What are you talking about?" Rielle's smile grew and she did not even flinch as her eyes turned silver and Solidus took control.

"She is saying, Borsa, that I am still very much alive." Borsa fell back a pace in shock.

"No, you can't be. You died and faded away. It was witnessed!"

"Faded away, yes." Solidus said. "But I am far from dead. And now I have returned to make good on the promise I made you." Borsa regained some of his composure.

"And what promise was that?" Solidus stared flatly at the priest.

"I warned you to sever your connection before the Blood Moon Cycle. I warned you that, if you did not make that decision, I would return and make it for you." Even though the priest's face had been disfigured by the chaos, Rielle could still see an inkling of fear play across it. Borsa drew himself up.

"I have bonded with a great and powerful demon. You no longer have the strength to stop me." Then Borsa shouted in pain and clasped his head between his hands. A crack, like a bolt of lightning, shook the temple. Solidus waited patiently until Borsa had recovered before speaking.

"And yet, you struggle to keep the seal that binds the demon to you. You do not have access to its full powers yet, and won't for some time to come." Borsa growled.

"I have more than enough power to destroy you."

"Enough." The voice seemed to echo from all around them. Borsa went slack for a few moments and then stood straight, his eyes an angry, burning red.

"My host is not so used to his position." Borsa stated in a

low and raspy voice. "And he does not know the limits of his strength just yet." Solidus nodded.

"And he is very foolish." Borsa chuckled, the sound grating across everyone's ears.

"I cannot argue. Though I think all humans are foolish, so it makes little difference to me." Solidus nodded again, seemingly without emotion.

"Having changed his seal so that you can speak with me directly shows his lack of understanding. But it seems I have gotten ahead of myself. I would know your name." Borsa bowed low to the ground.

"I am called Latriamadorialith. You may call me Dorialith if it suits you more. I know human tongues often stumble over our names." Solidus nodded yet again.

"Very well, Dorialith. Now, it seems we are at an impasse. I obviously cannot simply stand idly by and watch you grow in strength as your seal becomes more permanent. And I am sure you would like nothing more than to avoid my destroying you." Borsa straightened again.

"This is true. The Priest's body may not be ready to control my power yet, but you are also within the confines of a body not your own. You may have the strength to send me back to the chaos once again, but it would take much time and concentration, neither of which you have to waste." Solidus sighed.

"As much as I do not like it, you are also correct."

"What!?" Segine burst out. "You have all the time in the world, why not just kill him and get it over with?" Borsa chuckled again.

"Because, young knight. Even as we speak the spirits and creatures of the Telatian wastes stir and struggle to find their way here. Should your fine master Solidus try to gather his power to send me back, it would immediately attract those spirits here. I would, of course, fight to stay in this realm and make sending me back to the chaos take that much longer. In which time those spirits will arrive and tear you all apart. Master Solidus will be too weak from fighting me and he will not be able to protect you and you would all die." Borsa smiled triumphantly. Segine could not find words to convey his frustration.

"But you have a proposal to make." Solidus stated. Borsa nodded.

"Indeed. As you know, I am no match for you in my current state. Even in time, as Borsa becomes more capable of handling my powers, you will have the power to send me back to the chaos at your whim. However, it could burn out your host to do so. My suggestion is this. Why not go our separate ways? I will take my host and prepare him to harness my full powers. You may do the same with yours so that she may be able to withstand your powers as well. In time we may meet again, on a more level field of battle. Then you may do as you see fit without risking the lives of your companions. And, of course, to be fair I would not take any major action until that time." Segine grunted in disgust.

"We will not make any deal with filth like you."

"I accept your terms." Solidus answered. Segine's mouth gaped open and he stuttered angrily, unable to form complete words.

"Is that wise?" Vesth asked. Solidus nodded.

"There are factors at play here that you cannot yet understand. This is our best course of action." Borsa's grin nearly split his face. "It is refreshing to finally confront a human who can make a rational decision. I respect that. In return I will give you fair warning. I will be leaving here momentarily by way of my own power. Once gone, you will have only a few minutes to leave before the spirits rush in and overwhelm you." Solidus nodded.

"And in return for your warning I will give you one of my own. Be wary of what you plan. The next time we cross paths, there will be no bargaining. There will be no retreat, and there will be no escaping your fate. Should you not cause any problems before that time, I may send you back to the chaos. If you go forward with your plan to destroy this world, I will destroy you utterly in kind." Borsa's grin did not lessen in any way.

"I eagerly await the time we meet again." Borsa's body went limp and when he straightened again, his eyes were a sickly yellow.

"It seems my demon will not lend me the power to fight you. He seems to think that you may be able to overpower me at this time. So I am afraid I must leave you now. Maybe next time we meet I will be allowed to confront you."

"Be careful what you wish for Borsa." Solidus stated coolly. Borsa frowned and nodded, then his body began to fade.

"NO!" Nysisset yelled, yanking a knife from her belt and rushing the fading priest. Segine tried to reach out and grab her, but he was not quick enough and she slipped away. She plunged forward and sank the knife deep into the priest's side. Borsa merely glanced at the knife as he would a speck of dust and then back at Nysisset. "Foolish girl." Without raising so much as a finger, Borsa's power threw Nysisset across the room and smashed her against the wall. Nysisset slid down the wall and landed limply on the floor. Borsa's body continued to fade.

"Next time your fate will be the same, Pravin Solidus." The last words echoed around the room as Borsa disappeared from sight. Solidus sighed.

"Segine, gather Nysisset quickly." Segine glared at Rielle.

"How can you act so calmly!" He roared as he hurried to Nysisset's side to check her. "She may be dead and you could have..." Solidus stared dangerously at Segine and the knight's mouth stopped working.

"Do not argue with me." Solidus stated quietly, though his voice conveyed an anger and power that reminded Vesth of the dragon Tiamat. Segine gritted his teeth but carefully lifted Nysisset into his arms and stood. Solidus moved Rielle to the center of the room.

"Come closer, they are already drawing near." Segine stepped into the center of the room and waited quietly. Vesth did the same, but his ears picked out just the faintest hint of something from outside the temple walls.

"I hear something." He said, looking back at the doors through which they had entered the room.

"Keep them out of your mind. It is the spirits who have already traveled here and are searching the city for us."

"How are we going to get out then?" Segine asked, a little testily. Solidus didn't look at the knight.

"Just be silent and hold still. We will be gone very shortly." Segine scowled and looked back at Nysisset. She seemed to still have color in her face, although very little, and he hoped that meant she was still alive. Rielle's eyes closed and power caused the air around them to ripple. Segine felt a horrible sensation of being torn apart and put back together again and found himself standing outside the doors to the Temple of Fire and Earth. The doors opened and Marina rushed out, several monks in tow.

"The spirits howl in anguish. What is happening?" Rielle shook her head and opened her eyes, back in control of her own body again.

"It is a long story, Mistress Marina, but right now Nysisset is badly hurt and in need of healing." Marina drew close and saw Nysisset in Segine's arms.

"I warned her not to act against Solidus's wishes. I hope it has not caused her permanent harm." She placed one hand beside her neck and then on her forehead.

"She is still alive, but she is in bad shape." She turned to Rielle. "Follow me inside, we need to prepare for her healing, and the monks will need to give you tea that will boost your strength before the strain Solidus put on you catches up with your body. Segine," She looked at the big knight.

"The monks will show you where to take her, then you and Vesth must go down into the town beyond this trail. There is someone there who you must bring here at once. You will know who they are when you meet them."

"But," Segine started.

"Do as I say!" Marina growled with the same anger Solidus had shown not moments before, though on a lesser scale. Without waiting for more words, she turned and rushed inside, Rielle in tow. The monks motioned for Segine to follow them and Vesth propelled him forward.

"Hurry, leave her in Mistress Marina and Rielle's capable hands. We have our own duties to perform. One cannot argue with, or comprehend, such power as they wield." Segine nodded blankly and followed the gesturing monks into the temple.

* * *

Vesth looked carefully over everything and everyone in the small town. There were a small number of vendors in the streets, trying to sell their wares to those few who walked the streets.

"Keep your eyes open." He told Segine, and glanced back to make sure the knight had heard. Segine nodded sullenly, staring blankly ahead. Vesth sighed quietly to himself and headed towards the street that served as a small market place.

He moved slowly, partly so he could carefully study each person they passed, and partly so he wouldn't lose Segine. They made it from one end of the street to the other, ignoring the vendors and their cries.

"Can I interest you in an odd or an end young man?" Asked an old man in a large hand cart at the end of the street. Vesth shook his head.

"No, we are here to find someone, not to buy."

"Oh?" The old man seemed amused. "Who are you looking for? Perhaps I might be of some assistance." Vesth shook his head.

"I do not think so, as I am not yet sure who we are looking for." The old man chuckled.

"How can you look for someone if you don't know who they are? It seems a folly to me." Vesth shrugged.

"Perhaps, but we were told we would know them when we met them. And I have not witnessed the failure of these sources as of yet." The old man nodded as if agreeing to some philosophical truth.

"Yes, indeed failure is not much of an option. It seems there is still no one foolish enough to argue with my elder brother and sister. Though I cannot blame you." Vesth took pause and considered this statement. The old man laughed.

"You are a sharp one Captain. Not many listen so closely to the ramblings of an old man." Vesth frowned and nodded.

"It is in my nature." The old man continued to laugh.

"So it may well be. But listening and understanding are two very different things." Vesth shrugged again.

"I do not need to understand. It is for others to understand. I am here merely to follow my orders and do my duty."

"Ah." The old man said, amused at this. "Duty to order one's heart. I am sure it gives my brother no end of grief."

"Make sense old man." Segine finally spoke. The old man frowned mockingly. "And I thought a knight was meant to be gracious and courtly. Surely you have not forgotten all those years of training for knighthood have you, Sir Segine Memoria?" Segine's eyes narrowed.

"How do you know my name?" He asked suspiciously. The old man frowned and tried to meet the knight's gaze, but soon could not keep a straight face and started chuckling again.

"What I know, and how I know it, is not for you to know." Segine growled and Vesth placed a restraining hand on his shoulder.

"Come now," The old man said in a hurt voice. "Worry for your friend should not degrade your manners in this way. Your worry is misplaced, knight." Segine turned his back to the old man and said nothing. The old man smiled.

"My brother and sister will revive Nysisset, I assure you."

"You are Gartiel Delgorin, aren't you." Vesth stated. The old man smiled, then disappeared and reappeared next to Vesth, offering his hand in a handshake.

"Very good Captain, I am surprised you remembered my full name after hearing it only once." Vesth looked at the old man's hand and then took it in a brief handshake.

"I am good at remembering names." Segine continued to ignore the old man. The old man's smile wore off.

"Do not blame Solidus for what happened to the girl, Sir Knight. She was warned, by several, not to act against Borsa. She let her anger and lust for revenge blind her and she ignored the words of her elders." Segine growled and started to walk away, but was stopped as the old man appeared before him.

"Do not take this lightly, Boy." The old man carefully enunciated the last word. "There are forces at work here that are dangerous just for humans to bare witness to. Every action we four take, especially Solidus, has a specific purpose. It is not for you to understand that purpose, you need only follow the instruction given you."

"We could have ended this fight before it began!" Segine shouted. "Instead, Solidus bargained with the enemy and let him escape."

"Watch your tongue!" The old man shouted back, and suddenly he seemed to tower over the Knight and did not seem so old and helpless anymore. Vesth began to feel like the four Alenon mages were not people to be trifled with. Segine stood in silent shock.

"You already know the reason why he did that. If he had fought, and killed, Borsa and his demon, you would all have died with him." Segine set his jaw.

"A necessary sacrifice to save the rest of humanity." The old man shook his head. "You don't get it yet, do you? You still haven't figured it out. It wouldn't have just been you." A questioning look flitted across Segine's face. The old man sighed.

"Solidus told you that there were forces at work you did not understand, you should be happy leaving it at that. But I can't let you jeopardize what Solidus is trying to do because you think you know better than he." Vesth frowned.

"What forces were he talking about?" The old man's eyes never left Segine.

"Did you not notice that no one remained in Tyr' Anon?" Vesth remembered the empty windows and streets, food left uneaten, and weapons discarded.

"So?" Segine asked snappishly.

"So?" The old man repeated in kind. "Where do you think Borsa got the power to seal the demon inside him without the aid of the Blood Moon Cycle?" Segine's eyes widened and understanding dawned on Vesth.

"He killed them?" The old man shook his head.

"No, he did something far worse. He fed on them, their very essence. Absorbed every ounce of power from them until they completely faded away. In the same way Solidus burned away his essence to save Rielle, Borsa burned away those in his city to fuel his own ambition." Segine was speechless, and Vesth had to fight to bring the words to his lips.

"What did that have to do with Solidus not fighting Borsa?" The old man finally looked back at Vesth.

"You already know that causing something to cease existing is a serious crime for magic users. Burning away their essence is almost as bad. When one of these magical laws is broken, it weakens the ties that bind the elements together. The area around Tyr' Anon was so weakened, that if Solidus had opened a pathway back to the chaos to banish Borsa and his demon, the path could have torn open and swallowed the entire city, possibly all of Telatia. Balance in the world would be lost, and the world as you know it would cease to exist." They were all silent for a moment.

"Isn't that what Borsa wanted? To destroy the balance in the world? Why didn't he do it then if it was so close?" The old man scoffed.

"For one thing, Borsa is a fool. Secondly, Solidus is extremely powerful. He could, possibly, have kept control of the pathway and banished Borsa. Or more likely, in Borsa's mind, Solidus would simply have destroyed him, tearing him apart without ever risking that pathway. However, Solidus chose the best option placed before him. By letting Borsa go he bought all of your lives back, and gained the time to prepare for a final confrontation without the risk of unbalancing the world." The old man looked back to Segine.

"Tell me now, knight, in his place, knowing what he knew, would you have made any other decision?" Segine struggled with himself, and Vesth could see he desperately wanted to say yes.

"No... I would not." He said quietly. The old man nodded.

"I thought not. Remember this the next time you don't agree with Solidus's decision. He can see far more than you can possibly imagine. Even as much as I can see, he still sees far more." Now the old man smiled again.

"Well, let's get going. As soon as Nysisset is taken care of we will need to be ready to move out."

"Already?" Vesth asked. "Where do we need to go?" The old man shrugged cheerily.

"I haven't the slightest idea. I am only the means of transport. There are places in this world only Solidus remembers, and I could not even fathom what wonders he may lead us to. All I know is that it is a place so dangerous, so ancient, so utterly powerful, that Marina is very upset that he has chosen to awaken it. And I don't know if either of you ever had older siblings, but I am not near so senile as to get in the middle of an argument with mine."

4

❧

Chapter Four

Rielle carefully tied the final bandage in place and stepped back from her work, wiping a thin film from her forehead.

"Finally done." She said with a sigh. Marina nodded as she turned to wash her hands.

"Yes. For a few moments there, I was afraid we might lose her." Rielle shivered as the stress of the last hour settled over her.

"I don't think Nysisset would have given up that easily. She is too stubborn to die." She said, trying to smile. Marina smiled in return.

"Indeed. I only wish we had had the time to take her to Agamemnon. He is a much greater healer than I." Rielle nodded.

"Solidus feels much the same, but he is pleased with the work we did." Marina nodded.

"Solidus is too kind, I am sure. Is he recovering well?" Rielle paused for a moment before answering.

"Progress is slow, but he is confident that he will be well in time." Marina sighed. "I wish he would not choose this path." Rielle shrugged.

"He says it is the only way to keep the balance. And that it is necessary for what must come." Marina shook her head.

"I do not envy your burden." Rielle tried to look cheerful.

"I am sure all will be well. But it doesn't help not to know what he is planning." Marina opened her mouth to speak, then shook her head and closed it again. After they had cleaned up, and made sure Nysisset was comfortable, Marina motioned to the door. "Someone is here, and I think it is time for you to meet him." Rielle looked at Marina questioningly, but followed her from the room without speaking.

They followed the various halls and passages, stepping aside for the occasional monk, until they came to the Temple's main door. With a motion from Marina, the monks at the gate pushed the bars aside and opened the door. Rielle walked out into the late afternoon sunlight and found Vesth and Segine listening to an old man beside a large peddler's cart.

"The price is right if you are interested. I am sure it would help you a great deal on your journeys." The old man said, holding up a small wooden box.

"Stop trying to con them. They can get everything they need from the monks here and it won't cost them a single coin." Marina stated loudly. The old man pouted and slipped the box back into a compartment on his cart.

"You ruin all my fun sister." Marina smiled knowingly.

"You make it too easy brother." The old man smiled and they embraced for a short moment.

"It has been a long time since you last visited." Marina told the old man when they released one another.

"I am sure I was here just a few weeks ago." The old man said, scratching the beard on his chin. Marina laughed in amusement.

"Try thirty years brother." The old man continued to scratch his chin.

"Truly? It seems like only yesterday. I guess a loss of time like that can happen when you get my age." Marina firmly planted both hands on her hips.

"I'm older than you, and I have never had such a loss. And neither has Solidus for that matter." The old man frowned.

"Now that's not fair, sister. Solidus is connected to the balance of the world in every way possible. He couldn't lose time if he wanted to." Marina tapped her foot.

"And what about me?" The old man held his hands up defensively.

"Now now sister, you don't look a day over three thousand. You simply think too much about the time. It's not so important when you look at the big picture." Segine stared at Marina openly. Vesth was able to contain his surprise, but Rielle still saw it play across his face.

"It's not polite to stare, Sir Segine." Marina stated coldly. Segine quickly averted his eyes, but the surprise still showed on his face. The old man chuckled.

"Come now, didn't Solidus ever tell you how old he was?" Segine shook his head and Vesth spoke.

"It never seemed like we needed to know." The old man looked at Rielle.

"And you?" Rielle nodded.

"I asked him when we first met, he also did not think it was important. He did, however, indulge me with an answer." The old man shook his head.

"Everyone always leaves out the little details. Well I am going to come right out and say it. I am two thousand eight hundred and eighteen years old. And I still feel like I'm in my hundreds." The old man flexed his arms to display his youthfulness.

"You go ahead and make a fool of yourself then. A woman never reveals her real age." The old man laughed.

"Come now, big sister, it isn't anything to be ashamed of. You are only six hundred years older than me." Fire flew from Marina's fingertips and the old man disappeared just in time to avoid being set aflame. Segine was staring again.

"Keep staring and I may do the same to you, Sir knight." Marina said scathingly. Segine quickly turned away and Rielle saw the hint of a smile on Vesth's face.

"I do not think we have yet been properly introduced." The old man stated from beside Rielle. Rielle jumped in surprise and shakily took the hand the old man offered her.

"I am Rielle Toriel Lyvinius of Hortaal." The old man shook her hand heartily.

"A very great pleasure to meet you, Rielle. I am Gartiel Delgorin of Alenon." Even in this old man, as carefree and happy as he seemed, Rielle could see just a touch of sadness when the name, Alenon, passed his lips. Rielle bowed her head.

"It is an honor to finally meet you, Master Delgorin." Delgorin chuckled.

"There is no need for that 'Master' business, I am but a humble trader. I am no great teacher like Marina or Solidus." Rielle smiled.

"But you are a powerful mage. One as venerated and power-ful as yourself deserves the title of Master to be placed before their name." Delgorin laughed.

"Oh I do not think so. How long was it before Solidus broke you of the habit of calling him master?" Rielle's cheeks flushed slightly and she tried to hide a smile. Delgorin nodded.

"Not long, I thought as much. And what is this venerated business? Go ahead, you can say it. I'm old." Rielle shook her head.

"No, I could never do that. Besides, that would be an insult to Master Solidus and Mistress Marina as well." Delgorin chuckled again.

"So it is 'Mistress' Marina now is it? There is a very crucial difference between her and I though. She may be older than me, but she sure doesn't look it. I mean, look at that full, glorious, hair. Her eyes, sparkling with youth. The beautiful glow of her skin." Delgorin ducked under a back-handed swipe from Marina.

"Quit your prattling." She told him, but a smile brightened her face. Delgorin stood straight and placed a hand over his heart, lifting the other in the air as if swearing a solemn oath.

"Every word of it is true. I am just an old, wrinkly, bag of bones." Rielle did her best to refrain from laughing as she watched the old man go off on a one sided conversation about beauty and age.

While Delgorin talked, and Marina corrected him on several points, Rielle could see that Segine was tense. Vesth saw Rielle, followed her eyes to Segine, then turned back and nodded with a frown.

Rielle slipped around the two ageless mages and quickly went to stand next to Vesth. He answered her thoughts without her having to speak at all.

"He still worries for Nysisset's safety. And I do not think he has come to terms with the way recent events have played out." Rielle nodded and glanced over at the gloomy knight. Segine stood, with his back to everyone, oblivious of the conversations going on around him.

"How old is Master Solidus?" Vesth asked. Rielle glanced at him and smiled.

"I don't think that is exactly an important thing to know is it?" Vesth shook his head.

"No, but recent words have brought about my curiosity. Did you have any real need to know when you asked?" Rielle's smile broadened as she remembered her initial shock when hearing Solidus's age for the first time.

"Perhaps not. It is not, however, my place to say. All you need to know is that he is very old. He was born before the Age of War." Vesth's cool exterior fell for a moment, but he quickly recovered.

"The Age of War began over three thousand years ago, and it ended a thousand years ago at the beginning of the Age of Peace." Rielle smiled innocently up at Vesth. "Did it really? Interesting." She quickly moved away to leave him to his thoughts and went to stand next to Segine.

"Is everything alright, Sir Segine? You look unwell." Segine blinked, but wouldn't make eye contact.

"I am well." He stated simply. Rielle stepped around in front of him so he would have to look at her.

"I am sure you are, but you worry a great deal. Is it for

Nysisset that you worry?" Segine didn't answer, but Rielle watched sadness, pain, and guilt all play across his face. "She is resting." Rielle told the knight. "Marina and I were able to bring her away from immediate danger. When she has rested enough, and is able to wake, we will leave. Where we are going we must travel to by boat, and Solidus plans to stop at the Temple of Alenon along the way. That way Agamemnon can look into her health. He is a much greater healer then Marina and I. He healed you before, when you were badly injured, remember? So you know he can be trusted to help her." Rielle watched as some of the pain was eased from Segine's features. Rielle smiled knowingly.

"Perhaps you should go to her. It would be wise to have someone watch over her in case something happens and more healing is required." The fog lifted from Segine's eyes.

"Perhaps you are right, Miss Rielle. It would be the honorable thing for me, as a knight, to stand guard over one of our own while they recover." Rielle nodded.

"Of course it would. But please, you do not need to add titles to my name. I am only Rielle." Segine finally met her eyes.

"It would not be proper for me to address you without a proper title." Rielle took hold of Segine's broad shoulders and turned him around.

"We are not in a setting that requires us to be proper, Segine. I will break you and Vesth of this obsession with proper words and acts. As we are, you should not let your duty blind you to what your heart tells you. Now," She said, giving him a light push in the back. "Go inside and check on Nysisset. The Monks can show you were she is resting. Try not to wake her by moving around too much, your armor rattles terribly." Segine half turned back and looked at Rielle. She made a shooing motion with her hand nodded towards the temple door.

Rielle watched in satisfaction as Segine gave her a defeated look and headed towards the temple. Vesth joined Rielle as Segine left and stood, arms folded across his chest.

"Did you hear me?" Rielle asked him. "I will break your habit of properness before we are through." Vesth shrugged and watched as Marina and Delgorin argued about the proper times to wear colorful clothing.

"If you feel like you must try, then I have no reason to argue. But my duty will remain the same." Rielle sighed.

"And this duty business will be the first to go." Vesth shrugged again, but the hint of a smile touched his lips.

"As you wish, Miss Rielle." He placed extra emphasis on the word 'miss'. Rielle scowled, but let the subject drop. They stood watching the two mages argue back and forth for several minutes before Rielle spoke again.

"I never knew there was so much about clothing that could be argued over." Vesth nodded his agreement.

"They are likely to be at this for some time." Rielle shook herself and slipped her arm through Vesth's and started leading him towards the temple.

"Very well then, they can stay out here and argue all night if they wish. But right now I am in need of a warm meal. Then you can help me warm up my sword arm." Vesth gave no argument and allowed himself to be led through the temple's doors and down the long hallways into its depths.

* * *

"Take the message urgently." Segine told the monk. The

little bald man nodded and quickly left the room. Segine turned as Nysisset moaned again. He quickly stepped to her side and watched as her eyes fluttered open.

"You are awake." Segine stated, unsure of what else to say. Nysisset blinked a few times and looked around the room.

"Where are we?" She asked.

"We are in the Temple of Fire and Earth. Are you well?" Segine stood beside the bed helplessly.

"Of course I am." Nysisset grumbled. She struggled to sit up and flinched as pain filled her senses.

"I've never been better." She insisted through gritted teeth. "What happened?" Segine told her the events following her attack on Borsa. Nysisset swore.

"Borsa got away." Segine nodded, some of his anger surfacing.

"Master Solidus let him escape." Nysisset looked at Segine, irritation plain on her face.

"Of course he did. That was the plan from the moment we stepped into the city." Segine was obviously confused.

"But why? He could have destroyed Borsa and we wouldn't have to keep on fighting." Nysisset sniffed.

"It's not that simple. Nothing is ever that simple. I've seen Solidus destroy creatures that stood in his path. My master told me stories of the many battles in which Solidus fought, mercilessly defeating his enemies when he was committed to the fight. If he let Borsa go, then he had a reason." Segine struggled to understand.

"But if you knew Solidus had a reason for letting Borsa go, why did you attack him." Nysisset growled.

"Because he took from us and I wanted revenge. His lackey killed Tiasia and I want him to pay for it. Dearly." Nysisset wobbled in her bed.

"You should be resting." Rielle said as she and Vesth entered the room. The monk that had delivered the message, as Segine had instructed, followed behind.

"Everything is taken care of here." Rielle told the monk. "It would be wise to inform Mistress Marina that Nysisset is awake." The monk bowed his way out of the room and closed the door behind him. Rielle turned her attention back to Nysisset.

"You shouldn't be sitting up yet."

"I'm fine." Nysisset said in irritation, her face growing pale. Rielle placed one hand on her back and one on her chest and forced her to lay back against the pillows. "You are not fine, not yet. When we got you back most of your bones were broken and you were bleeding internally. We almost lost you several times before we could get you stable." Nysisset sniffed scornfully and tried to sit up again. Rielle gently pushed her back down.

"You are not completely healed yet. Wait until you have regained some of your strength before you try to move around. We are going to take you to a stronger healer. When he is finished you will be well enough to move under your own power again, no sooner." Nysisset struggled.

"I will not lie here while that pig, Borsa, still draws breath."

"You will lay there until you are well enough to walk or I will tie you down or post Segine here at all times to hold you down if need be." Rielle said forcefully. Nysisset looked at Rielle in un-welcomed surprise and Segine inched closer to the door. Rielle stared Nysisset down for a few seconds before nodding.

"Good, I'm glad we understand one another." Rielle meant to say more, but a sudden wave of dizziness caused her to weave and Vesth quickly stepped forward to steady her. Images flooded her mind and it took her a short time to recover.

"What is wrong, miss Rielle?" Segine asked in worried tones, also stepping forward in case Vesth needed assistance.

"I am fine." She said, carefully lowering herself onto a stool, Vesth's hand under her arm for support. Nysisset watched Rielle carefully, daring to sit up as much as she could.

"It seems I am not the one we should be worrying about."

"Make her lie still, Segine." Rielle said, her head resting in her hands. Segine stepped to Nysisset's bedside obediently. Nysisset glared at him and all he could do was shrug helplessly.

"What is going on in here?" Marina asked, entering the room with Delgorin in tow.

"You should be laying still, Nysisset." Nysisset grumbled defeatedly and laid back against her pillows.

"What is wrong Rielle?" Marina made her way through the crowded room to Rielle and knelt on the floor before her.

"What is happening?" Head still in hands, Rielle leaned forward, Vesth's strong but gentle hand holding her upright, and mumbled a few words into Marina's ear. At first Marina's eyes widened and then set as she heard the words Rielle spoke. She quickly turned.

"Delgorin, get it open immediately." Delgorin nodded without a word and left the room quickly. Marina called for several monks to enter the room and directed them to lift Nysisset onto a stretcher.

"Take hold of the stretcher, Sir Segine." Marina commanded, motioning with her head as she grasped the opposite end. Segine did as he was told and helped Marina carry Nysisset from the room. Vesth helped Rielle to stand and then supported her as they followed the knight.

They made their way outside where they found Delgorin thrusting two long poles into the ground about fifteen feet apart. Each pole had a ribbon, inscribed with characters no one recognized, attached to the top and fluttering in the light breeze. Everyone stood and watched as the old man worked and then ushered his cart into position before raising his hands above his head. The ribbons at the tip of each pole shivered, causing a ringing sound like the toll of a tiny bell. As the ringing grew louder, light spread down the poles to the ground and filled the space between them. The light blurred and twisted until it formed a picture.

Gone was the path down the mountain. In it's place was a broad road, lined by trees as far as the eye could see. Delgorin lowered his hands and took hold of his cart.

"Let's go." He said simply, then pulled his cart through the light and onto the tree lined road. Both Vesth and Segine hesitated at the sight of this magical gateway.

"Walk through to the road." Rielle told them.

"It will be no different than walking through an open door." Vesth nodded and slowly walked through the light, supporting Rielle's every step. As he passed the two poles, Vesth flinched, remembering the feeling of passing through the portal from the Mercury Mountains to Alenon. But, to his surprise, Vesth felt only a cool breeze as he passed between the poles and he made his way to Delgorin's cart where he leaned Rielle against its wooden frame to let her rest. He turned to find that the mountains were gone, replaced by miles of low hills and forests. Vesth watched as Marina coaxed Segine through the light, the big knight squeezing his eyes tightly shut.

Once they were through, Delgorin passed by them and waved his hand through the air in front of him and the light between the poles blurred and faded away. Delgorin took down his poles and lashed them to the side of his cart. Rielle checked Nysisset's bandages while Marina directed Delgorin to clear space in his cart where they could place Nysisset's stretcher. Delgorin grumbled and began tossing things off of his cart, the items disappearing into thin air halfway through their flight.

Eventually a space was cleared and Delgorin directed them to place Nysisset carefully inside, at the same time muttering something about 'bad business'.

"Please, Master Delgorin." Segine faced the old man once Nysisset was made comfortable.

"Please allow me to pull your cart until we reach our destination." Delgorin looked Segine up and down with a critical eye.

"Normally I would refuse you outright young knight. But seeing as we are in a hurry, and in light of the fact that most of my valuables have been... removed." Delgorin's gaze shifted to Marina for a moment. "I do not think there is much that can be broken by rough hands if I were to let you pull the cart for a short time." Segine bowed deeply without a word and then placed himself at the head of the cart. Vesth helped Rielle onto the back of the cart, where she sat down next to Nysisset's head, then turned when he saw Marina motion to him. She whispered a few words to him and he nodded before turning and heading down the road in front of them.

"You may proceed Sir Segine." Marina told the knight. Segine nodded and bent, taking hold of the carts handles and lifting. The knight grunted a little under the weight, and the muscles on his arms stood out. The knight leaned his weight against his arms and the cart groaned into motion. Delgorin fell into step beside Marina.

"So, sister, What is it we shall do?" Marina, though outwardly calm, scanned everything with a critical eye.

"I will accompany Solidus to Alenon and aid Agamemnon there. I would advise you to do the same, but I know you will not." Delgorin smiled.

"I never really liked the confined spaces of the temple. I am much more comfortable out roaming." Marina nodded, the slightest of smiles touching her lips. "Then I suggest you keep on the move and out of sight. There are things looking for us. Search for anything that will give these young ones an advantage." Delgorin glanced at Marina.

"Didn't you already give them the..."

"Yes." Marina cut him off. "But I do not know that Rielle yet has the strength to use it. She is strong, and intelligent, but it may be some time before she can control It's power." Delgorin nodded.

"And even if she can, she has companions who are at a severe disadvantage to the task they have before them." Marina nodded and they walked in silence for several minutes.

"I am going to make sure we are not followed." Marina

said, dropping back from the cart. Delgorin stopped and half turned.

"Be careful what you do. The world is not ready to have magic re-introduced to it just yet. I do not think you want the attention anything flashy will bring." Marina frowned.

"I am not so foolish little brother. They will be searching for us, now that we have escaped them. And once I am safely within the walls of Alenon, they will hunt you all the harder. We cannot afford a mistake now." Without further words, Marina turned and started off, back the way they had come. Delgorin watched her go for several seconds before hurrying to catch Segine and the cart once again.

It was not long before Vesth was seen rushing back down the road towards them. Segine pulled the cart to a stop as Vesth approached. Vesth nodded to Segine as he passed and quickly moved to the back of the cart to stand before Rielle.

"We have a problem." He stated, slightly out of breath. Rielle's face paled, seeing worry in his face.

"What is it?" Vesth blinked at her then looked ahead, down the road and beyond their line of sight.

"Port City is under siege."

5

Chapter Five

Vesth returned to the camp and joined the others around a small camp fire.

"Men in armor guard each road leading to the city and a large force camps before the gate." He reported.

"Who are they?" Segine asked. Vesth shrugged.

"They all wear plate armor that bears no insignias, and their full helms cover their features. It will not be possible to identify who they are or where they are from." Delgorin and Marina leaned in and began whispering to one another.

"I feel a taint in the air." Rielle said quietly, staring into the fire. "There are Nibilus nearby." Segine sat upright, alert to their surroundings, and Vesth placed one hand subconsciously on his sword.

"Are the soldiers Nibilus?" Rielle shook her head.

"No, they are human. But the Nibilus are nearby, waiting for the city to fall." "The humans are also tainted." Delgorin stated. "It is possible some of them are hosts, but it is more likely they have been in contact with the Nibilus." Marina nodded her agreement. Vesth's features darkened.

"Regardless, we need to get into the city if we want a ship to sail us to Alenon, or anywhere else for that matter." Rielle stood suddenly.

"There is a way. A small passage on the east side of the city. It is a group of tunnels that run beneath the city streets that protect the city from flooding with sea water." Vesth scratched at the ground with a stick.

"Those tunnels are narrow and winding, barely wide enough to walk through. Not to mention it is a thousand feet of open ground from the forest to the city with armed guards and an army camped on its doorstep. There is no way we could get Nysisset into the city that way in her current condition. And we would be unable to take Master Delgorin's cart with us at all." Everyone looked to the cart where Nysisset lay quietly asleep.

"I will take her." Delgorin volunteered. "I can take her some distance from the city and when you have acquired a ship we can meet somewhere on the shore and you can retrieve her." Vesth scratched his chin.

"That is a sound plan. There is a small cove to the west of here. It is secluded, the beach is bare, and the forest is near enough to hide in. I believe that would be a suitable place to meet." Rielle nodded.

"I agree, that is a suitable place."

"I will go with Master Delgorin to help protect Nysisset." Segine stated, rising to his feet.

"No." Rielle responded firmly. "We need your help finding

a ship to carry us to Alenon. Master Delgorin is more than capable of protecting Nysisset in the mean time." Rielle motioned for the knight to sit. He did so, looking forlornly at the cart where Nysisset lay. Vesth nodded.

"Very well then, now that we are settled on a plan, we should see to its details." "Be careful not to get too caught up in planning." Marina said. "It is easier for those who are watching to see what you will do if you plan every move first." Segine harrumphed.

"A good strategist always plans five moves ahead. In this way he knows how each move will progress and how each piece will move and respond." Marina nodded.

"Your schooling has not been poor Sir knight. A Good strategist does always plan many moves ahead. But, a Great strategist only plans one move ahead. The difference is, the move the Great strategist plans will always be the right one. And it is easier to adjust your strategy if you only have to change one move for each obstacle you encounter." Rielle nodded and looked to Vesth. Vesth looked between Rielle, Marina, and Segine before nodding.

"I agree. It would be best to plan each move as we come to it. We do not know what we will encounter in the city and we will make fewer mistakes that way."

"Then we first have to figure out how to get to the tunnels without being seen." Rielle stated.

"Leave that to me. "Marina said. "I will make sure no one sees us." Segine shuddered.

"More magic." Marina smiled.

"There is nothing wrong with magic, Sir Segine." Segine shuddered again, but said nothing more.

"Once we get to the tunnels I should be able to get us through them into the city." Rielle stated. "I toured them once, as a young ambassador in training."

"And you are confident that you can remember the way?" Marina asked. Rielle nodded. Vesth tossed the stick in his hand into the fire.

"Once inside the city, I have a contact who may be able to help us with a ship. I wouldn't exactly call him reliable, but he owes me a few favors and I think I can talk him around." He told them. Rielle nodded.

"Good. I think that is as far as we need to go. We can play the rest by ear once we get into the city." Marina nodded her agreement. Rielle's eyes glazed over for a moment as she focused inwardly. Both Marina and Delgorin sat straighter and watched Rielle intently. Several moments passed by and Rielle finally shook herself and blinked a few times.

"What did Solidus have to say?" Marina asked. Rielle looked around their small camp, trying to will her eyes to see beyond the trees and deep into the forest.

"Solidus says we need to tread lightly. Something is not the way it should be." Marina and Delgorin nodded slightly and Delgorin stood.

"I will take Nysisset to the west and wait for you to arrive with the ship." Marina stood and followed the old man to his cart. They whispered quietly for a few moments and then Delgorin took hold of his cart and pulled it toward the road.

"Wait." Came the faint call from the back of the cart. Rielle quickly stood and rushed to the cart.

"There is something you need to find in the city." Nysisset

muttered. "Since I will not be entering the city it has to be you." Rielle nodded.

"What do I need to find?" Nysisset coughed to clear her throat and winced slightly.

"An artifact. It was taken during one of the few successful incursions by humans into the Mercury mountains. During a 'Witch hunt'." Nysisset snorted in derision.

"A small silver amulet set with a pitch black stone. It was taken by someone who lived in this city, and I can feel it's presence here still. It makes itself precious to those who carry it, so they will not have given it away or sold it." Nysisset found the strength to reach out and take hold of Rielle's arm.

"With it my strength will grow from the weak shadow it is now into an all consuming darkness." Rielle could see a feverish light behind Nysisset's eyes, almost begging to be given the power she spoke of. Rielle carefully took Nysisset's hand and removed it from her arm.

"I will search for it as much as I can before we leave the city." The fevered expression passed from Nysisset's eyes and she nodded and laid back against her pillows. Delgorin resumed his pace and was soon out of sight. Rielle watched them go and then returned to the small fire.

"How long will it take you to prepare?" Rielle asked Marina.

"An hour, maybe a little more." Rielle nodded.

"Around nightfall then. That should be the perfect time to slip into the city." Vesth stood.

"Then we should all prepare. I will go keep an eye on the soldiers and return just before full dark." He made a shallow bow and then headed off into the trees. After watching him go, Marina turned to the remaining two.

"I would suggest you two rest, and maybe get some sleep. I have a feeling this will be a long night." Segine nodded and stared sullenly at his feet. Rielle looked into the fire for a few minutes and then unrolled her bed roll and laid down to follow Marina's advice.

* * *

The time passed quickly and Rielle got little rest before she was awakened by Vesth's gentle nudge.

"It is nightfall." He told her, when her eyes had fluttered open. Rielle forced herself out of the depths of sleep and sat up.

"Is everything ready?" Vesth nodded and stood from where he had been crouched. "We are all packed and ready to leave, save for you, and Mistress Marina says she is ready to do whatever it is she is going to do." Rielle nodded and quickly got to her feet, rolling her bed roll and tying it to her small pack.

The last bits of sunlight were fading from the horizon and the only illumination in the camp came from a small lantern in Vesth's outstretched hand. The fire had been extinguished and all evidence of their camp had been carefully swept away. Segine stood off to one side, quietly waiting while Rielle quickly packed by the light of Vesth's lantern. Marina came into the circle just as Rielle hoisted her pack onto her back.

"Everything is in readiness. We may leave at anytime." Rielle nodded, and then stopped as pale white mist drifted through the trees from behind Marina, as if following her into the clearing.

"Soon the fog will roll fully in from the sea and our advance will go unseen." Rielle nodded again and then lead the way toward the beach. As they entered the trees, the fog hit them like a wave. One moment the way was clear and they could see their way clearly through the trees by the pale light of the rising moon. The next moment the fog fell over them and everything; sound, sight, smell, and touch, was swallowed by it's presence. Each of them was no more than a pace behind the one ahead, and still the fog swirled thickly between them.

When they reached the open sand of the beach, the fog grew dense and heavy, making it difficult to breath. Rielle turned and gathered the other three into a group and spoke quietly, her voice muted by the fog.

"We will stay as close together as possible and walk in the water at the end of the beach so that the sea will erase any sign of our passage. When we reach the city wall we will follow it until we find the drain and then enter the city. Is everyone ready?" Everyone nodded but no one spoke. Marina looked drawn and tired. Vesth was alert and his sharp eyes scanned the blank fog around them. Segine was uncomfortable in the unusual fog, but it was obvious that his mind was on other things. Rielle did her best to contain her sigh and then turned to lead the way.

Vesth's hand landed on her shoulder and gently pulled her back. Rielle opened her mouth to complain about his action when he placed one finger against her lips to silence her. They waited for several seconds and then muffled voices could be heard through the fog.

"Soldiers." Vesth barely breathed the words into Rielle's ear. She nodded and Vesth let his hands drop from her shoulder and lips. Vesth took the lead and the others followed closely behind. They waded knee deep into the lapping ocean tide and then followed the beach in the direction of the city.

Their progress was slow, as they could often hear soldiers laughing gruffly a short distance from the shore and did not want to attract attention by splashing. Once they could even see the faint glow from a campfire not more than fifteen feet from the shore. Vesth traveled with his sword loosed in its scabbard and one hand placed firmly around it's hilt.

By the time they had reached the city wall, the ocean water had seeped through their boots and their clothing clung with the moisture from the fog, thoroughly soaking all of them. Rielle placed one hand against the wall and began following it deeper into the water. She was waist deep before she felt the shallow crevice that housed the grate for the drain. A slow trickle of water drained through the crevice and quickly soaked anything that was not already wet.

Vesth slid up to Rielle's side and she motioned to indicate the drain. He nodded once then climbed up onto the ledge and tested the grate just beyond. Rielle winced as she heard a sharp squeal and then Vesth motioned for them all to follow. Vesth assisted everyone into the drain and then replaced the grate and took his place at the rear of the column.

Rielle led the way, trying to find her way in the dark, not daring to create any light to see the way. She placed one hand against the wall which was covered in slick brine and other things she did not wish to think about. The drain was very narrow and Rielle could hear Segine scraping his shoulders against the walls every so often. Eventually Rielle's eyes adjusted and she could make her way by what little light leaked into the tunnels from the street drains above.

She twisted and turned, following her mental map to the

place she had chosen to go above ground. Eventually she stopped and did her best to look out of the drain above her head.

"I think this is the place." She whispered.

"Segine, I need you to try and pull the grate out quietly and lift me up high enough to climb out." Segine nodded mutely and Rielle stepped back to let him get to the drain. Segine took hold of the bars with both hands and pulled with a loud grunt. Nothing happened. He struggled for several seconds then looked to Rielle and shook his head. Rielle's eyes glazed for a moment and then she drew Solidus's sword and held it out to Segine.

"Use this to pry and break it loose." Segine took the sword and looked at it uncertainly.

"Don't worry," Rielle said, motioning for him to continue. "You won't break that blade." Segine still didn't look like he was sure he liked the idea, but slid the edge of the blade along the edge of the grate until he found a place it would sit.

Once it was in, Segine set his shoulder against the sword's handle and heaved against it. The grate creaked and dust and bits of hardened salt broke free of the wall around the drain. Segine reset the blade into a better position and then pushed against it once again.

The grate squealed and broke loose, nearly falling to the floor. Segine caught the falling edge of the grate and pulled it down, handing the sword back to Rielle. Rielle wiped it off on her tunic and returned it to its scabbard before motioning for Segine to lift her. Segine took hold of Rielle's leg, with an uncomfortable look, and lifted her high enough to reach the drain and look out.

Once she was sure that no one would see them, Rielle wriggled up onto the street then looked back down into the drain and motioned for the others to follow. Segine stepped back and let Marina use his leg as a step up and Rielle pulled her up onto the street. Vesth easily pulled himself out of the drain and then turned back and reached into the drain to help Segine. Rielle looked around the streets.

"We are in the poor district." She told Marina quietly. "No one should care about a few more poor souls wandering the streets." Marina nodded.

"Indeed, we should decide what we are doing next though. It won't do us any good to wander around blindly."

"We should split up." Vesth said, standing up and brushing off his clothes as Segine replaced the grate. "A group of people wandering around the city during a siege will attract attention that we don't want right now." Rielle nodded and Marina spoke. "Agreed, what would you suggest?" Vesth looked at his surroundings.

"I would suggest two groups. One to go to the docks and find the boat we need, the second to find the captain of that ship and convince him to leave the port while the fog is still over the water." Marina nodded.

"I agree, but we should hurry. The fog will only last until the sun rises and we want to be gone from this place by then." Vesth nodded and looked to Rielle.

"Well?" Rielle frowned as Vesth shifted leadership to her.

"I think you and I should go find this contact of yours and convince him to sail. Marina and Segine can go wake the crew on the ship and get them to prepare the ship to sail for when we get there." Vesth nodded.

"I agree." He looked to Marina and she nodded as well. "The ship you are looking for is small and fast, which suits us, and is called The Voltaire. When the watch asks who sent you tell them it was me. I am well known to this particular crew and they should do everything you ask them to." Marina nodded and without further questions she turned and headed back towards the sea.

"Come Sir Segine, we must be ready before the night is through." Segine nodded blankly and followed without question. Rielle watched them go through the swirling mist and disappear.

"I hope Segine can snap out of this unhappiness, we may need him soon if all does not go according to plan." Vesth nodded.

"I am sure he will pull through, but right now we have our own task to focus on." Rielle nodded and turned back to Vesth.

"Then lead the way. I do not know where to find your friend." Vesth nodded and turned to follow an alley before walking out into the rest of the city, Rielle close behind.

6

Chapter Six

Rielle wrinkled her nose at the filthy man laying face down on the floor of the small house.

"Don't think he will be much use to ya Vesth." Said a plump little woman beside the man. She looked at him with disgust and shook her head, wiping her hands on her dirty apron.

"He was gone from home for a long time and got back right before the siege. He got depressed, drowned hiself in the bottle when he got here. But, If ye can get him up and moving hes all yours. I don't need him moping around here all day when he should be out looking for new cargo. The siege will end eventually and he better have hiself cargo by that time or I will take him out and drown him with my own hands." Vesth half bowed.

"You are too kind madam." The woman nodded once.

"And don't ye forget it. And while I am on the subject, ya don't visit as often as ye should either Vesth." Vesth smiled.

"I have been rather busy of late. I will strive to visit more often." The woman nodded again but then smiled.

"I will get ye some food while ye try to wake up that oaf. The two of ye look like ye could use a good meal." Vesth nodded and muttered a thank you before kneeling beside the comatose man, slapping him a few times.

"Wake up, Strolm. I am in a hurry, so don't make me resort to less pleasant devices." The man stirred in his drunken sleep, but did not wake. Vesth sighed, then took the man by the collar of his shirt and lifted him off the ground before tossing him across the room. The man landed with a heavy thud on the floor before rolling against the wall. The man groaned and sat up blearily, trying to open his gummed shut eyes.

"What'sh goin' on 'round heresh?" The man tried, unsuccessfully, to stand and just ended up leaning against the wall. "Didsh we hit a reef or shomething? We aren't under attachk are we?" The man reached for something at his hip and tried to stand again.

"You aren't under attack Strolm, Not yet anyway." Vesth stated, crossing his arms over his chest. The man called Strolm turned toward the sound of Vesth's voice and again tried to open his eyes.

"That you Vesh? I haven't sheen you in a while, what are you doing on my ship?" Vesth took a vase of flowers from a small table and threw the water straight into Strolm's face. The man gasped.

"Wake up you old fool, you aren't on your ship. You have been at home drinking for three days." The water, as well as the man rubbing it off his face, finally loosened his eyelids enough to get them open. He peered around the room with blood-shot eyes.

"Clair ish going to be angry with me." He stated after a few seconds of thought brought him back to the present.

"Very." Vesth agreed. "But I have a job for you and she should cool down before you get back." The man looked up and tried to focus on Vesth.

"A job? Doesh it pay good?" Vesth shook his head.

"No, I am calling in a favor. My companions and I need to get somewhere, and you are going to take us." Rielle nodded and Strolm seemed to notice her for the first time.

"Ooh, Your companion there ish very pretty." Vesth shrugged.

"Don't let Clair see you looking at another woman." Strolm's eyes sharpened and snapped over to look at the kitchen door and then back to Vesth.

"Well, I am sorry Vesth, I would love to help you out but I am tight on money and I can't afford to sail without cargo." Vesth shook his head.

"Not good enough Strolm. You owe me, remember? I am not going to let this one go, It is too important. Or should I tell Clair and my companion here just why you owe me so much?" Strolm Sobered almost instantly.

"That is low, Vesth." He said, rising to his feet with a grumble. "What is the job?" Vesth nodded and motioned to Rielle. Rielle took a deep breath and locked eyes with the man across the room.

"We have a companion who is injured and cannot travel with us without a ship. We have two destinations, which will be revealed to you after we depart. If absolutely necessary, I will have you and your crew compensated for your time."

Strolm eyed Rielle up and down, gauging her strengths with an expert eye.

"You want me to sail, without telling me where we are going, without payment up front, and with no idea why? Sounds like bad business to me." Vesth nodded.

"Be that as it may, those are your terms. We must leave tonight, before the sun rises." Strolm let out a harsh, grating sound that Rielle assumed was a laugh.

"Now you want me to sail at night. What have I done to you to deserve this Vesth? No, don't answer that. Since you are not going to let this go, and you seem set on suicide, Then I have no choice but to do as you ask. But after this you and I are even, you hear me?" Vesth nodded.

"Clearly." Strolm let out an aggravated sigh and rubbed the bridge of his nose. "Fine, how many passengers?"

"Six"

"Any cargo?"

"Possibly a small cart, nothing else."

"Distance to destinations?"

"Three days one way, at least. Plan for five." Strolm sighed again and looked up. "Well let's get going then." Rielle closed her eyes for a moment and then spoke. "Our companions have been instructed to wait at your ship, we have other business to attend to before we depart. We shall meet you at the docks shortly." Strolm swore under his breath.

"This keeps getting more and more complicated." Vesth nodded again.

"You have no idea." Strolm waved a hand through the air.

"Fine, fine, go do whatever you want. I have things to do if you want to leave before sun up." Strolm stumped off towards the kitchen door.

"CLAIR!" He roared as he stepped through the door. Arguing floated through from the other side as the door swung closed. Vesth turned and led Rielle to the door and they stepped out into the night air.

"What is next?" He asked. Rielle pointed towards an enormous mansion, barely visible in the fog.

"Nysisset asked me to find something for her, and Solidus says it would be a good idea to see if we can find it before we leave. The Governor's home should not be too far from here, and that's as a good a place to start looking as any."

"If ye be going to the Governor's Manse then ye will want to be in something that is not so dirty as what yer wearin'." The woman Clair spoke through the open doorway as Strolm stomped angrily from the house.

"If ye have need of some proper clothes there is a seamstress who lives just down the way. Stop in and tell her I sent ye and she can put the cost of the clothes on my tab." Vesth bowed at the waist.

"Again, you are too kind." Clair harrumphed.

"Just make sure ye stay fer supper next time 'round. Bring the pretty lady with ye too." Rielle blushed and Vesth nodded before turning and leading the way down the street.

"If we don't leave now, she may well think of something else we need." He muttered to Rielle as they hurried along. Rielle smiled and continued to hurry along the darkened streets.

"We should take her up on her offer though." She stated. "We would look out of place in the Governor's home the way we are now, and I do not think we want that much attention." Vesth nodded once and turned down a street corner and stopped in front of a small building with a wooden sign depicting a faded spool of thread. Vesth hesitated for a moment before stepping forward and knocking quietly on the door.

* * *

Rielle stood regally before the Manse door and pulled a silk bell string, causing a light tinkling sound inside. Vesth shuffled uncomfortably in his new velvet jacket.

"Be still." Rielle told him. "We don't want to give them the impression that we are anything other than what we seem to be." Vesth grumbled but stilled himself and stood at attention. The large door slid open noiselessly, and an old gentleman stepped out and inspected them.

"What purpose brings you here so late this evening?" He asked. Rielle nodded at him as she would a lowborn servant.

"I am an ambassador from the High King. I arrived here shortly before the siege began and I wish to speak with the Governor on a subject I find most distressing." The old man looked at Rielle suspiciously.

"If you are an ambassador from the High King, why have you not come here sooner?" Rielle snorted haughtily at the man, as if he had suggested something despicable, and waved a hand at him, making sure he saw her signet ring.

"I was only to stop here on my way to Gentry to speak with King Yisu. I had hoped that this siege would be dealt with before I had to spend any significant time here. But this detracts from the point, I am distressed and I will speak with the Governor immediately." She turned her nose up with a pout and the old Gentleman hurriedly apologized. Vesth stood still, surprised at the skill with which Rielle plied her trade.

They were ushered inside and led to a waiting room where Rielle sat importantly on an upholstered couch and Vesth stood beside her as if he was her personal guard. It was not long before they were again escorted to another room before a pair of doors were opened for them and they were allowed into a large study where a middle aged man sat at a neatly organized desk. Rielle could immediately feel a dense darkness emenating from the man.

"Please, come in." He said, with a small wave of his hand. Rielle walked in as naturally as if it were her study they had entered. The man at the desk removed a slim pair of spectacles, placing them on a stack of parchment, and rose to greet her.

"It is always an honor to speak with High King Morien's ambassadors. What brings you here this night?" Rielle nodded politely and slid gracefully into a soft chair before the Governor's desk. The Governor also sat, and Vesth took a place behind and to one side of Rielle.

"I had hoped this siege would be done with sooner than it has, But it may have provided us with a unique opportunity." The Governor folded his hands on his desk and leaned forward attentively.

"And what is this opportunity you speak of Ambassador?" Rielle waved her hand, as if motioning to everything in the room.

"My mission, though I cannot speak of it in full, Is to speak with King Yisu on the war with Telatia." The Governor nodded.

"Of course, but I had thought all aggression on the part of Telatia had ceased after the night of the Blood Moon. With the Great Gates impassable it was understood that the threat from Telatia was minimal." Rielle nodded.

"Yes but, as the siege outside your gates attests, the war is far from over. We believe they are biding their time so they can re-gather their strength for another push. It may take weeks, or months, to mine through the rubble of the great gates, but we believe they still intend to fight." The Governor gave his clasped hands a troubled look.

"I can see the logic of your conclusion, I am only sorry that this siege prevents me from speeding you on your way. However, with soldiers on the beaches, there is no way a ship can safely leave port." Rielle nodded.

"Indeed, but again, this same circumstance has left us with a unique opportunity we may have otherwise overlooked." The governor's eyes returned to Rielle.

"Ah yes, this opportunity you spoke of earlier. What, pray tell, is this nuance you have found in such a dire seeming situation?" Rielle smiled innocently.

"I remembered something from my studies, something I may have overlooked if I had not had the time to sit waiting for the siege to end." The Governor nodded dutifully and waited for her to continue.

"I remembered that at one point one of your ancestors, your Great-grandfather I believe, made a successful witch hunt into the Mercury Mountains. I believe it is the great deed that earned him the position as Governor here." Rielle noticed the Governor's eyes darken almost imperceptibly. The man nodded.

"Indeed, he loved to tell the tale to my father before he passed. What of it?" Rielle took a fraction of a moment to straighten her dress and think before replying.

"It seems to me that if your Great-grandfather could make a successful attack on such an evil place, he must have done so with some great skill, or something else that might help us in the fight against the obvious evil's of Telatia." Rielle could see that the Governor was trying to hide the tension growing in him. He still managed to nod and reply thoughtfully.

"Indeed, if such a skill or strategy was known to me, I would most assuredly entrust it to you to use against the Telatian Demons. But, unfortunately My Great-grandfather passed away when I was very young, and if he ever spoke of it to my father then he took it to his grave as well." Rielle felt a light touch on the back of her shoulder as the Governor spoke. She nodded slightly to signal Vesth that she had heard the Governor's words as well. Rielle turned her nod into a pout and spoke again.

"That is indeed unfortunate. Do you know if he left anything behind that might help us? A journal, notes, perhaps even some item he might have carried with him?" Rielle saw the Darkness in the Governor's eyes sharpen instantly at the mention of an item.

"No." He stated emphatically. "And I am not sure I would let you have my Great-grandfather's... Journal if he had had one. I feel as if you are attacking my family's honor." Vesth again touched Rielle's shoulder at the almost unnoticeable pause the Governor had made." Rielle quickly bowed her head.

"I do apologize if anything I have said seemed like an attack.

I am merely trying to find a way to help our kingdom in its time of need." The governor didn't seem to relax as he stood.

"And I apologize for my outburst. I did not mean any disrespect towards a trusted ambassador of our King. This siege has just worn me down I suppose." Rielle also stood. "Of course, I understand completely. It is difficult to be in a position of power when times are hard. I am sure the King will commend you for your strength and leadership when this war finally comes to an end." The governor nodded and smiled tightly.

"It is my honor to serve." Rielle smiled in return, but a small voice sounded in her head.

"*You won't help him any by side-stepping the issue.*" Solidus told her. "*It will eat away at him and corrode his soul, leading him to an early grave, as it did his father. It is not something that was meant to be in human hands. Signal Vesth to be ready, then confront the boy.*" Rielle's smile lessened. She carefully stepped away from her chair and touched Vesth's hand lightly. He immediately stiffened and his hand slid carefully over his sword. Rielle turned again to face the Governor.

"Consequently, Governor, I happen to know that your Great-grandfather returned from the Mercury mountains with a relic. A trophy, as you will, to prove his prowess on the battlefield." The man's false smile fell from his face and the darkness in his eyes intensified. Rielle locked him down with an imperious stare and continued.

"It is not something that should be in the hands of humans. It should have remained in the mountains that forged it. It's taint has brought darkness to this place. And attracted the eyes of those who would use you." Anger and fear flashed in the man's eyes, confirming what Rielle had guessed.

"The priest's of Telatia have come to you already, haven't they? Promising to give you power beyond your darkest dreams in exchange for your service." The Governor snarled and his hand clutched at his chest.

"It was given to me, It is mine and no one else's. The stupid priests believe they can control me, but when they make me a host It will give me the power to destroy all of them and take control of the world as they cannot." Vesth's hand tightened around his sword, but Rielle shook her head, and he instead stepped in between her and the Governor.

"Don't you realize you cannot control such a thing yourself?" Rielle said, locking her eyes with the Governor's, forcing him to look at her and listen. "Don't you realize that hosting a demon will burn away your soul and leave nothing but an empty husk?" Uncertainty flashed in the man's eyes before hatred replaced it.

"You can't trick me, I know you want it for yourself." He growled, almost to the point of shouting. Rielle shook her head.

"It is not too late, you still have time to let it go, and heal the damage it has done to your soul. You can still return to being the powerful leader the people of this port need." Just the slightest hesitation in the man's demeanor gave Rielle hope.

"Please, for your sake and the sake of your people, let the Amulet go." Rielle's hope was shattered as the man was filled with Rage.

"You shall never have my Amulet. Never! It was given to me. It's Mine! No one shall have it but ME!" Rielle sadly shook her head.

"Then you leave me no other choice. Vesth, take it from him, he is wearing it around his neck." The man's eyes widened in fear and hatred. "But please, try not to harm him. He needs to live to realize it was never his to keep. And the people here need a leader, even if it is a corrupt one." Vesth nodded and walked around the desk and towards the man cowering behind it.

"It's Mine!" The Man shouted once more before leaping at Vesth, teeth bared. Vesth calmly sidestepped and struck the man across the side of his neck just below his jaw. The man's eyes rolled back into his head and he dropped limply to the ground. Vesth hauled him off the floor and laid him back into his chair before taking hold of a gold chain around his neck and yanking it free. He returned to Rielle's side and held it out to her. Rielle took the chain and pulled the small amulet from Vesth's grasp.

It was a simple, roughly rounded, disk of silver with an onyx black stone that had been pressed into the metal while it had still been hot. Rielle felt as if the chain in her hand was covered in rancid pitch and shuddered, fighting the urge to drop it.

"It is the evil you feel. Forged by Khornal himself to strengthen his servants in the age of power, his power still permeates it. You would do well to keep it somewhere that will not come into physical contact with you, or you will risk becoming indentured to it as this unfortunate boy was." Rielle nodded and slipped it into a pouch at her waist.

"Let's go. We have much to do tonight." Vesth nodded, and they walked from the room, leaving the Governor unconscious in his study.

* * *

"I really don't like the look of this Vesth." Strolm said, trying to look out over the water, still obscured by mist.

"I am just as uncomfortable with this as you Strolm, but we have no other options to get past the siege." Strolm grumbled and stumped back over and pushed the pilot away from the wheel.

"Spotters, keep your poles forward." He called, trying to keep his voice low. "Don't want to run aground on the reef before we get into the cove." A half dozen men rushed around the bow of the ship, thrusting long wooden poles into the water as the ship crept forward. Signals were given and Strolm made adjustments each time to steer clear of obstacles. They reached the cove just as light was starting to appear on the horizon.

"We must move quickly." Marina told everyone. "The fog will begin to fade and will disappear entirely with the rising of the sun." Everyone nodded, but Rielle turned towards the beach.

"Something is not right." Everyone froze, trying to peer through the fog to the sandy beach ahead. Rielle shuddered and Marina jumped onto the rail on one side of the ship, raising her hands in the air.

"Everyone get down!" She yelled as the air around her rippled. All at once a half dozen lights flashed from the shore and several fiery projectiles hissed overhead. Most of the crew dropped to the deck as Marina deflected two of the projectiles and evaded a third. Rielle leapt up beside Marina and Vesth drew his sword.

"That will not do you much good here." Marina said, indicating the sword. Another projectile shot between Rielle and Marina. Vesth raised his sword, twisted elegantly, and split the projectile in two. An arrow fell to the deck with a hiss and Vesth flicked his sword to remove any residue.

"You were saying, Mistress Marina?" Marina smiled.

"Well, it seems I have misjudged you soldier."

"Save your praise for later sister." Solidus spoke from where Rielle stood, weaving her hands intricately before her. "We have enough to deal with before us now." Marina nodded and turned back to face the beach.

"As you say brother. It seems that the art of magic is not as lost as the people of this world would like to believe." Rielle nodded.

"Indeed, but they cannot form the magic alone, they must bind it to an object to harness it's power. Thus the arrow that Vesth so deftly cut from the air." Another set of flashes filled the beach with light. Marina brought up her hands but Rielle shook her head.

"I have this one." More projectiles shot through the air towards the ship. Rielle's hands rose and a wall of purple energy formed in the air, covering most of the ship in a protective cloak. The projectiles struck the wall with a sharp ringing sound and fell into the sea. Rielle winced as the force of the enchanted arrows pressed against her.

"Where is Delgorin, the old fool." Marina scowled.

"No need for such a face sister, I am present and accounted for." Delgorin appeared just behind Vesth, Nysisset cradled in his arms, breathing heavily.

"Segine, take Nysisset below deck." Marina ordered, jumping down from the rail and rushing to Delgorin's side. Segine quickly did as he had been told and took Nysisset from the old man's arms.

"What happened?" Marina asked, ready to catch the old man if he fell. Delgorin waved his hand dismissively.

"I am fine sister, just old and worn. We reached the cove with relative ease and I set up a small camp just inside the trees to wait for you to arrive with the ship. But it did not take long for us to be discovered." Marina gave Delgorin a strange look and the old man nodded.

"There were Nibilus and a Basilisk scouring the woods for who knows what. They came across us and I only just had the time to shield myself and the girl. The Nibilus themselves were not difficult to dispense with, but the Basilisk was another matter. On top of that, the longer we stayed, the more of them started to show up. Soldiers came too, and creatures wearing robes. They are the ones sending that annoying light after us." Another volley of projectiles broke against Rielle's shield and fell into the water.

"How long can you hold that shield Rielle?" Marina asked, turning as she spoke. Rielle shook her head.

"Not through many more attacks, but probably long enough to get the ship out to sea." Marina nodded and turned back to the crew lying on the deck.

"You heard her." Marina shouted commandingly. "Get this ship out to sea, double time." Some of the men stood shakily and moved to do as they were told, but many of them remained face down on the deck. Marina drew breath to shout again, but was beaten to the punch by Strolm.

"Get your sorry hides off this deck and get this ship to sea!" He roared. "Or the beating I will give you will make you wish you had been struck down by magic!" The men scattered, leaping from the deck and rushing to haul lines and tie the sails with an energy that surprised Marina. The ship began to turn and glide across the water towards the mouth of the cove.

"We aren't out of this yet." Delgorin muttered, pointing towards the shore. Through Rielle's purple tinged shield they could see a single light on the beach, growing steadily with each passing moment. Marina growled like a feral cat.

"Delgorin." The old man nodded and began muttering to himself and turning slowly in place. Marina rushed to Rielle's side, but did not reach her by the time the large light shot towards them. The enormous projectile smashed against Rielle's shield, shattering it and throwing her backwards off the rail. Marina jumped and just barely managed to catch Rielle before she landed head first on the deck. Rielle did not stir and Marina placed one hand against her cheek.

"Poor thing burned up all her energy." Marina gingerly set Rielle down and jumped back onto the rail. More light was building on the beach.

"Let's see you deal with this." Marina scowled and spread her feet into a wide stance, placing her hands to one side and concentrated her will into her hands. Dark purple energy filled the space between her hands and grew to encompass her. The light on the beach again shot towards the ship. Marina slid her feet together, her hands in front of her, and pressed her gathered power into a single point before her.

A purple bolt of power shot from her hands and met the light from the shore mid flight. An explosion reverberated through the air and sent out a shockwave that threw water into the air, obscuring sight and knocking Marina off balance. She fell backwards off the rail, but twisted and managed to land on her feet. She looked up and another projectile of light shot through the mist towards the ship. Marina took in a sharp breath of surprise and rose to try and stop it. But before she could act, the projectile impacted a solid silver barrier. Marina's eyes opened wide and whirled around to see Rielle standing with one arm raised, her eyes shining with brilliant silver light.

"Solidus." Marina nearly gasped. Rielle's head turned slightly to look at Marina, and it was almost as if an image of Solidus cloaked her entire body. Solidus spoke, No hint of Rielle's voice marring the sharpness in his.

"They channel the power of the Basilisk and it's Nibilus horde. This is not a battle we can win without harming innocents in the area around the cove and nearby villages." Marina nodded.

"Then we must flee." Solidus nodded.

"That is our only course of action. But it must be precisely done, lend Delgorin your strength and I will deal with those on the beach." Marina wasted no time rushing to Delgorin's side and stretching her hands out toward him, purple energy beginning to stream from her and into the old man as he continued to mutter and turn. Solidus walked slowly towards the rail at the side of the ship and waved his hand negligently.

The fog parted and the morning sun beamed through to glitter on the disturbed water of the cove. A terrible collective cry reverberated over the water from the beach as the black haired Basilisk leapt into the protective cover of the forest and several Nibilus writhed on the beach, burning up in the morning light. Ten figure's stood on the beach, wrapped in sand colored cloaks, and gathered around a large mounted crossbow. Two soldiers were quickly pulling the bow back and loading it to fire again.

"Come." Solidus's voice echoed across the waters, though he had not spoken loudly.

"We will decide the outcome here and now while the Nibilus cower in the shadows and you must use your own power." The Soldiers were obviously affected by Solidus's voice and one even fell to the ground clutching at the large arrow he had been trying to place in the crossbow. One of the ten figures took the large arrow from him and pushed him aside, placing the arrow and stepping back to join his fellows. Solidus bowed his head.

"Then let us begin." Solidus turned fluidly in place on one foot and bent at the waist, waving his arms around him as if gathering the air itself into his hands.

The ten figures on the beach held their arms out towards the crossbow. Moments passed and then light began to gather from around them, traveling down their arms and filling the arrow with a twisted form of power.

The air around Solidus began to twist and gather as he pulled it into physical form.

The arrow on the crossbow began to hum and the bow buzzed, seemingly with anticipation to be fired.

As Solidus continued to twist and turn, the air began to take shape. Ten identical swords formed from the air and hung around Solidus like a protective curtain of silvery shifting blades that cut the very air from which they were formed.

The buzzing crossbow reached a fever pitch and then launched its arrow as an enormous ball of writhing energy.

Solidus stopped abruptly and sent his ten swords hissing through the air. The swords formed a circle and spun around a central point until they blurred the air with their speed. They slashed through the projectile and split it into innumerable pieces that continued to hiss through the air towards the ship. Solidus smiled and flicked his wrist and the ten swords continued their flight to the beach.

"Now Delgorin!" Solidus shouted. Delgorin came to a stop, opened his eyes, and thrust his hands into the air and called out with a power that flashed from the old man to encompass the ship and everyone onboard.

"Ut Templum Alenon!" A roar filled their ears as the projectiles reached them and the ocean exploded into the air around the ship.

The soldiers on the beach watched in horror as Solidus's ten swords pierced the ten figures around the crossbow. They stood still as the swords in the ground behind them faded away before each collapsed into a lifeless heap. The soldiers watched the magic users fall and then heard the ocean roar up around the ship. As the water fell back down again the ship had disappeared, leaving no trace it had ever existed.

The soldiers, unsure of what to do and with their leaders dead, turned and fled into the forest. Some to relay to the army what had transpired, most to return to their homes and hide from the terrifying powers they had just seen displayed.

7

Chapter Seven

What was left of the projectiles crashed harmlessly against a frosty white barrier that did not even ripple when it was struck. Brilliant yellow energy washed over the ship and into the sea where it slipped silently into the depths. Delgorin placed his closed fists together in front of his chest and took a deep breath. Then he slowly released his breath and straightened his arms until they lay at his side.

"Well done brother." Marina said quietly as she caught the tired old man and supported him.

"You did well brother." Solidus agreed, turning from the side of the ship and walking to stand beside Vesth, who had returned his sword to its scabbard. "And you will have plenty of time to rest as Agamemnon tends to young Nysisset and Rielle. Be sure that the sailors know the rules of the temple and assure them we will be leaving once again in a day or two." Solidus turned to Vesth as the energy around Rielle's body began to fade and her eyes started to dim.

"Take care of her Vesth, She will need tending when

Agamemnon has finished with Nysisset." Solidus's voice faded away and Rielle's eyes closed and she fell forward into Vesth's waiting arms. Strolm ordered his men to set a plank to the beach and then listened attentively as Vesth explained what was expected of him and his men before heading towards the temple.

"It may be best not to tell your crew exactly where we are. I am sure they have heard the stories, but I doubt any of them has ever actually seen the temple before." Strolm nodded.

"I agree. I don't much like it here myself, but it seems to me that it is getting just as dangerous in the rest of the world as it is supposed to be at this temple." Vesth nodded.

"Indeed, but as I explained, You and your men will be safe here on the ship as long as no one goes near the temple." Strolm nodded.

"Very well, go be done with your business here Vesth. The sooner we can leave and get this crazy voyage over with the better." Vesth adjusted his arms so that he could carry Rielle more comfortably, then nodded to Strolm and walked down the plank and up the path to the temple. Agamemnon was waiting for them at the temple doors when they arrived, several stretchers hovering beside him.

"I greet my elder siblings warmly." The old priest said. "But you do like to cause a commotion don't you." Marina smiled at Agamemnon as she helped Delgorin onto a stretcher.

"It is good to see you little brother." They shared a brief hug and then turned as Vesth and Segine placed their charges onto the floating stretchers.

"My my, you do seem to get yourselves injured often enough don't you." The old priest quickly checked Nysisset and Rielle.

"Well, young Rielle should be alright. Her energy is used up but, with her connection to Solidus, she should recover rapidly." Agamemnon turned back to Nysisset. "This one, however is going to need some attention."

"You like to run your mouth, don't you old man?" Nysisset grumbled. Agamemnon chuckled.

"You recover very well on your own little dark one. I think that you should be almost whole by the time you have left here." Nysisset harrumphed, but nodded.

"Then maybe these ninnies will actually let me stand on my own." Agamemnon chuckled again.

"I see Khornal still builds his servants with exquisite personality." A hoarse laugh came from Delgorin.

"I would say. She nearly complained me into a stupor by the time we reached the cove."

"I wouldn't have to complain if you had a softer wagon and didn't hit every root and hole in the road." Marina scowled.

"Hush, both of you. I swear, I am taking care of children." Agamemnon smiled patiently.

"Come now sister, you need rest too. They don't have much more energy to argue with anyway." The old priest turned and clapped his hands together. The two large doors swung open into the temple and the stretchers moved silently inside.

"Come, a meal will be served while I tend to your injured ones. I assume everyone remembers their way to the dining hall." Vesth and Segine nodded and Marina opened her mouth to speak.

"Come sister," Agamemnon spoke authoritatively. "You cannot live on piety alone. I have known monks who died trying just that. Our communion with Her may wait until I am finished tending to the young ones. And Delgorin should be fit enough to join us by then. She wishes to hear from all four of us. And it would be best if the young student was awake for it as well." Marina closed her mouth and half bowed to Agamemnon.

"I understand, High Priest." Agamemnon smiled again.

"Then come sister. If you are not hungry, you may come with me and tell me what has been happening in the outside world while I tend to the others." Marina nodded and followed Agamemnon into the temple after the stretchers.

"I guess that means we are on our own Sir Segine." Vesth told the knight as they watched the others disappear into the dimly lit temple.

"Indeed." Segine responded with a nod.

"But I cannot say I disagree with Mistress Marina. I do not feel much like eating." Vesth sighed inwardly.

"Nor I. Recent events have not set well with my stomach." Segine rubbed his shining breastplate.

"Too much magic to make me comfortable." Vesth nodded.

"I don't like it very much either. Though I have been convinced Magic is not an evil thing, I still do not like trusting my life to it." Segine sighed outwardly.

"I long for the days when one could rely on his sword and his skill to resolve any situation." Vesth placed one hand longingly on his sword, and one hand on something inside his tunic, over his heart.

"Hopefully that day will come again." He looked up and cleared his throat. "I will go to the dining hall and see if I cannot force myself to eat." He told Segine. "As the priest said, one cannot live on piety alone." Segine reluctantly nodded his agreement and followed Vesth into the temple.

* * *

Rielle's dreams were dark. Shapeless shadows drifting from place to place, speaking words on the edge of hearing. Rielle wandered, alone, through cold passages of stone and black mortar. The air around her becoming more thick and tainted the further she traveled into the heart of the mountain.

'Strange. I have never seen this place before, and yet, I feel I know it.' She thought to herself. She grasped at a velvety cloak draped around her shoulders. Continuing through each passage Rielle searched for something, but for what she was unsure. She rounded a corner and a twisted shape leapt at her, teeth bared and claws tearing for her throat. Without thought, she drew her sword and struck the creature down in mid flight. The creature landed on the floor with a thud and Rielle recognized it as a Nibilus. Curiously she looked to her hand and saw it holding an unfamiliar sword. It was an elegantly curved blade, similar to the one Solidus carried. It had carefully engraved filigree silver flowing across the blade like lightning and at its base stood a rearing dragon. The sword began quietly speaking words she could not fully understand.

"Put it away Rielle, do not listen to its whispers. The time has not yet come for you to wield this blade." Rielle turned to see Solidus approach her from a path leading away from the place she had been going.

"Solidus, what are you doing here?" Solidus smiled and carefully removed the sword from her hands.

"I am within you, I am everywhere you go, remember?"

Rielle looked at her empty hands for several moments. The slightest of memories brushing her mind, bringing her visions of a beautifully decorated room of flawless white stone. Rielle looked back up into Solidus's smiling face.

"Where are we?" Solidus slid the decorated blade back into the scabbard at Rielle's side.

"We are in a time and place far from now. A dream shared between us that gives you a glimpse of the future. But it is not yet time for you to start seeing these things. You must pass through numerous trials before you will be ready to read the balances in the fabric of reality." Solidus held out one hand and, after a few seconds pause, Rielle took it and he led her back the way he had come.

"So this is the future?" Rielle asked, looking around at the dark stone that surrounded them.

"A possible future, yes. But there are things that still must be done in the present. You must wake from your fitful sleep, young Rielle. Many others approach, and you must earn their blessings before you return to this place." They entered a small room, a bed in one corner. Solidus lead her to the bed and let her sit down on its surprisingly comfortable surface.

"There is much you must learn, much you must do, and so very little time to do it." Solidus told her, kneeling on the floor next to the bed and taking both her hands in his.

"You and the others must grow stronger. You must grow to be the champions that this world desperately needs. There will be a changing of the guard and you must all be ready when it comes. It will be you few threads in the balance that will determine the outcome of what looms ahead." Rielle looked into Solidus's eyes and, for a moment, she felt she could see everything. Everything that was and could possibly be. An infinite feathering of possibilities and a power so unfathomably absolute that it defied the mortal frame that contained it.

"You are beginning to see." Solidus's voice seemed far away and Rielle's eyes drooped as she began to feel exhaustion washing over her. "By the end you may even understand. But, for now, it is time for you to wake." Solidus stood and then supported Rielle's head as she lay back against the soft bedding.

"Your Trials await you young one." Solidus whispered, carefully pressing Rielle's eyes closed. "Be ready."

* * *

Rielle woke with a start and sat bolt upright. Something tugged at the back of her mind, begging to be remembered. Rielle knew she had dreamed, but she could remember nothing but a curved sword, a soft bed, and Solidus's gentle hands.

"It is good to see you are finally awake." A familiar voice shook Rielle from her fog and she looked around. She was sitting on a bed in a beautifully decorated room of sparkling white stone. Agamemnon smiled at her from across the room as he washed his hands in a shallow silver basin filled with clear water.

"You took longer to recover than I thought you would, But I suspect you might have more power than we expected. Using all of it was a stress your body is unaccustomed to." Rielle blinked a few times and then slid to the edge of her bed, suddenly feeling stiff.

"How long was I asleep?" She asked, rubbing her neck and shoulders in an attempt to loosen them.

"Only a few hours." The old priest said, drying his hands. "I only just finished mending your friend Nysisset. She is sleeping now and should be recovered by the morning." Rielle suddenly remembered the ship and the attack in the cove.

"So, we escaped?" Agamemnon nodded and made his way to her bed side.

"Indeed. Delgorin managed to transport the ship and its passengers to the safety of the temple. It took its toll on him, but he has always been a tough old soul and he will also recover quickly." Rielle nodded and tried to stretch her neck. Agamemnon gently pulled her hands down to her sides and then placed his hands on her head. A warm feeling flowed through Rielle from the old priest's hands, alleviating her stiff and sore muscles, and left her feeling refreshed. She took a deep breath and sighed. Agamemnon smiled as he stepped back so she could stand.

"It is good that you have woken. We must prepare you for the ceremony." Rielle looked up at the old priest, confusion in her eyes. Agamemnon smiled and motioned for her to follow him.

"We have been called to commune with our Patroness. She wishes to speak with all four of us. Since you now house Solidus within your body, you will have the honor of attending the ceremony." Rielle's eyes widened with surprise.

"How will you speak with her? Will she appear to you and speak with you face to face?" Agamemnon chuckled and shook his head.

"Unfortunately that is not entirely how it works. To keep the balance when Alenon fell, Necrotic Dracolich Khornal physically bound himself to this plane in order to keep his servants and their Evil sealed in the Mercury mountains." Rielle nodded.

"I remember. Solidus explained it shortly after our meeting with Lord Khornal." Agamemnon nodded.

"That is good. The binding was necessary to keep the balance. However since Lord Khornal, the Deity of Evil, is physically bound here our Patroness, the Deity of Good, may only manifest herself here spiritually. She cannot take physical form while Lord Khornal is bound here." Rielle followed the old Priest slowly.

"So you cannot even hear her speak to you?" Agamemnon nodded sadly.

"That is correct. However, since we are also bound to her in spirit as her servants, she can commune with our spirits directly while we are in her presence. When we are communing with her, you will be unable to hear her speak, but you will be able to feel her presence when she enters the Altar Room in the center of the temple. But even that small honor will fill you with an indescribable feeling. An experience none outside of Alenon have had for well over two thousand years." Rielle suddenly felt very tense, and very humbled at the same time. Agamemnon lead her to a small room lined with incandescently white robes.

"There should be clothes here that will fit you. I will leave you to your privacy and seek out Marina and Delgorin. When you are dressed, Solidus can guide you to the Central Altar Room and we may begin." Rielle nodded, and the Old Priest bowed himself out of the room. Rielle carefully sorted through the robes until she found one her size.

"There is a basin of water near the far end of the room where you may cleanse yourself before dressing." Solidus informed her. Rielle carefully draped the robe over her arm and walked towards the end of the room.

"What is she like?" Rielle asked aloud. Solidus had no need to ask who she meant.

"Kind and loving, and beautiful beyond compare. She has a forgiving heart and a strength that can be felt by all in her presence. Even the most malicious of beasts become calm, and tame when she is near." Rielle felt unconditional love flow from Solidus as he spoke.

"Even her twin Brother, Lord Khornal, Is kind and gentle when they are together. Though it has been a great many years since their last meeting. I hope, though it may be wrong of me, that the prediction of which you are a part truly is the final pre-diction. If complete balance was achieved in this world then She and her Brother could be reunited, and the Servants of Alenon could once again stand and bow in the light of her beauty and strength." Rielle finished bathing herself in the crystal clear water from the large basin set into the wall, and then carefully pulled on her new robe.

It was like nothing she had ever worn before. It was light and soft, as if a white cloud had been formed into cloth, and so smooth that Rielle thought it was likely that no dust or stain could possibly stick to it.

"The secret to weaving this fabric was lost long before even my time. But there has never been a single temple robe that has ever needed mending or replacement. It is rather impressive for some-thing that is even older than I am." Rielle felt one of her sleeves, carefully running a gentle hand down its length.

"Not even the finest of silks in the High Kings court could even begin to compare." Rielle felt Solidus smiling.

"Nothing I know of can. Come, the others are waiting for you." Rielle nodded and left the room. Following Solidus's

directions, Rielle found her way through the long sweeping halls of the temple to a small sitting room which housed two stunning opalescent doors.

Agamemnon stood before the doors, in an ornamental gold embroidered white robe, waiting with a quiet smile on his face. Marina and Delgorin were also there, each in white robes identical to the one Rielle wore.

"Now everyone is here." Agamemnon spoke, his voice carrying a strength and power that Rielle had only ever heard Solidus match. "The time of Communion is upon us. The call has come."

"And we shall answer it." Marina and Delgorin intoned together. The two opalescent doors swung open smoothly and noiselessly, seemingly of their own volition. Rielle had thought she had seen many wonders in her life time, but nothing prepared her for what lay inside these two doors. Rielle's breath caught in her throat as she entered and all she could do was stare.

The room itself was flawless white marble, polished so highly that the single tiny window far above them lit the room brighter than day. The room was perfectly round, with a smooth floor that nearly reflected the images of those standing on its surface. But everything else paled in comparison to the altar that graced the room across from the doors.

The altar stood waist high and was made from a single, perfect diamond that sparkled with a light that seemed all its own. Atop the surface of the altar stood two angels, also made of diamond, with their arms outstretched, as if beckoning all who saw to come to them. Rielle felt like the little angels could have moved and spoken had they chosen to. A tear formed in Rielle's eye as the doors behind them closed.

"I had almost forgotten how beautiful this room was." Marina said quietly, standing next to Rielle.

"The only part of the temple I have missed in all these years of travel." Delgorin admitted reverently.

"It may be best if I take over from here." Solidus said. Rielle nodded and Solidus moved into control of her body. Agamemnon stood before the altar, hands pressed together and head bowed.

"We Four, Guardians and loyal servants of Alenon, have gathered as our Mistress has called." Agamemnon's voice was soft and quiet, but made the room hum anxiously. Marina took a step forward and dropped to one knee.

"Taeldora Marina, Guardian of the temples of Galbrea, has answered her Mistress's call." Delgorin mirrored Marina and stepped forward, dropping to one knee.

"Gartiel Delgorin, Guardian of the byways of Galbrea, has answered his Mistress's call." Rielle felt herself step forward and kneel.

"Pravin Solidus, Guardian of the Balance of Galbrea, as well as his Student and Host Rielle Toriel Lyvinius, have answered his Mistress's call." Lastly, Agamemnon knelt and placed his folded hands upon the altar.

"Siguard Agamemnon, Guardian of Alenon and its Temple, has answered his Mistress's call. We four kneel and await the word of our beloved Patroness." As Agamemnon finished speaking the altar began to glow and a sparkling mist seemed to permeate the room. A single shaft of light shone down through the mist and touched the altar. Rielle's senses were suddenly filled with joy and comfort and the weight of a presence of such purity that after a few moments, Rielle knew only light.

8

Chapter Eight

It took Rielle a long time after they had left the Altar Room before she was able to think clearly again. She dressed mechanically and made her way to the dining room where lunch was served. She ate, not really listening as Marina and Delgorin conversed quietly with each other. Segine was nowhere to be seen and Vesth appeared only once to ask Agamemnon something before leaving again.

Rielle's head began to clear after she had eaten, and she decided to go check on Nysisset. Agamemnon told her where to go and she slipped quietly into the room where Nysisset was recovering. Nysisset sat in a straight backed chair beside the window, looking out over a small garden courtyard.

"I see you are feeling better." Rielle said as she closed the door behind her. Nysisset barely spared her a glance and shrugged.

"I feel the same as I always have, but my strength is returning rapidly. It pains me to say so, but the priest seems to know what he was doing." Rielle smiled and sat in another chair across from Nysisset and glanced out the window.

Vesth and Segine stood in the courtyard, each stripped down to their breeches, circling one another and trading blows. Rielle was not surprised to see that Segine was covered in large, clearly defined muscles. Despite his size, the knight stepped lightly and could react with speed when Vesth struck. Vesth was much thinner than the bulky knight, but his muscles were no less well defined, and he struck blindingly fast and blocked Segine's counter attacks with seeming easy.

"They have been at it for over an hour now." Nysisset spoke, her eyes watching the two men spar. "I admit that, for humans, their stamina is rather impressive." Rielle nodded her agreement.

"And they do not lack in skill either." Rielle stated after Vesth made a particularly intricate parry and managed to get around to Segine's back. Nysisset shrugged.

"Perhaps. Amongst other humans I imagine that they are considered very skilled. But humans have grown soft in the Age of Peace." Nysisset tried to sound scornful, but Rielle noticed a hint of a smile when Segine managed to spin around to block Vesth's attack from behind. Rielle smiled and chose not to speak. They watched the two men spar for another few minutes in silence before Rielle spoke again.

"I almost forgot, We managed to retrieve the amulet you wanted from the Governor at the port before we left." Nysisset looked at Rielle, keeping a straight face, but excitement showed in her eyes.

"Do you have it with you?" Rielle shook her head.

"No, Solidus left it on the ship. He worried that bringing

it into the Temple might do it harm. It is yours when we leave tomorrow." Nysisset nodded, her excitement not lessening in the least.

"I suppose that makes sense. Temples as old as this one have their own protections. Lord Khornal's Temple would destroy anything it saw as a threat entering its doors." Rielle nodded. And they continued to watch the two men sparring outside. They sat in companionable silence as they watched and it was not long before the sun began to set. Vesth and Segine ended their practice with a bow and gathered their things and made their way toward the temple doors.

"Will you be joining us for dinner?" Rielle asked, lifting herself from her chair. Nysisset shook her head.

"I will remain here. I hate to admit it, But I do not yet have the strength to wander from my room, and I refuse to accept help from anyone here." Rielle shrugged.

"Suit yourself, I am sure Agamemnon will bring food to you at some point anyway. And if you rest well tonight then perhaps you will have the strength to leave tomorrow under your own power." Nysisset gave a sniff.

"Of course I will. I am not so weak that I would need more than one night of sleep to stand." Rielle smiled.

"Of course. I will tell the others of your incredible powers of rejuvenation. I am sure they will be very impressed." Nysisset managed a short laugh.

"As they should be." Rielle laughed as well and opened the door and nodded her head.

"Good night, Nysisset." Nysisset nodded back after a moment's pause.

"Good night."

* * *

"You are sure about this?" Agamemnon asked. Rielle nodded and Solidus spoke.

"I am. The balance shifts and this must be the counter. By the end, many things that are sealed must be unsealed and this is the first step." Agamemnon half bowed.

"You are Balance Mage, and only you see everything as it must be." Agamemnon straightened and looked silently on for a moment before continuing.

"You are sure Rielle will come out unscathed? I know that our Patroness agrees with this, but is Rielle yet strong enough to survive such a thing?" Rielle nodded.

"Steps will be taken to ensure Rielle's body is protected. They will all be present." Agamemnon's features fell for a moment.

"All? Is that not taking a very great risk?" Solidus breathed a heavy sigh.

"It is, unfortunately, a risk we must chance. The changing of the guard cannot be complete without it." A hint of a memory stirred within Rielle at the mention of a change of guard, but it was swept away as Agamemnon spoke again.

"But all of them in one place? The weight will put great strain on the world." Rielle nodded again.

"Yes, but I will be focused on keeping the repercussions at bay. I am not needed for the ceremony. Besides, the Temple should absorb most of the strain." Agamemnon nodded.

"Of course. I am in agreement with Marina, but I will bow to your greater wisdom." Marina huffed moodily with her arms crossed in front of her chest. Rielle glanced at Marina and then at the others at the far end of the dining hall.

"Are you sure he is near?" Solidus asked suddenly. Agamemnon nodded. "Very. His waves beat at the barriers, straining to get inside. Even now it takes a great deal of concentration to keep the barrier from wavering. It is good that the Demons are afraid to come into his presence or I would be worried that they might try and attack the temple." Solidus sighed once again.

"He always has let his emotions rule him, even more so than Lord Tiamat. It is unfortunate, but a confrontation with him is inevitable."

"Can Rielle contain the power for such a confrontation?" Marina asked. "I must admit that Delgorin and I have gotten a little rusty over the years and we are not as strong as we once were. We will be little help until we have regained our former strength." Rielle nodded and Solidus spoke after a few moments thought.

"She is. She has grown quickly, and consistently pushing her own limits has extended her capacity to handle my power. She handled Lord Tiamat with very little backlash. Even with him in a fury, She should be able to handle Lord Leviathan as well. However, I hope I can talk him down before any such force must be used." Marina scoffed.

"I very much doubt it brother." Agamemnon chuckled.

"Lord Leviathan has a short temper, but he is reasonable when he can be made to see the facts. I am sure all will be well." Rielle nodded and the silver left her eyes.

"Then we will take our leave, we have a long way to go and Solidus says our time grows shorter." Agamemnon nodded with a smile.

"Come back and visit the temple again. And do be careful,

I hope I will not have to mend anyone the next time we meet." Rielle smiled and bowed to the old priest.

"I will do my best." Agamemnon nodded in return, and Rielle turned to leave the room, the others moving to follow. They walked down the path to the beach silently, no words passing between them. A plank was lowered onto the white sand and they boarded the ship. Rielle paused a moment to speak to a sailor, who nodded and disappeared below decks, before she turned and saw the Captain approach them.

"What course shall I set?" Strolm asked, obviously more than ready to leave. Rielle pointed out the direction.

"South-West. We will be sailing around the western tip of the continent." Strolm nodded without question and moved to the helm.

"Weigh anchor! Mainsail half forward!" He yelled, and his men leapt to obey his orders. The ship slowly moved away from the beach and started around the island.

"Captain, Have your men prepare for a storm." Rielle called up to Strolm. "Once we leave the protection of the Temple Island we will be in for a difficult ride." Strolm glanced down at Rielle as he guided his ship with a steady hand.

"Are you sure missy? It isn't the season for storms." Vesth sprinted up to join Strolm at the helm.

"Best not to argue with her Strolm. From what I have heard there may be something nasty waiting for us once we leave the calm waters." Strolm shrugged and turned back to glare down at his crew.

"Secure life-lines and batten down the hatches! Secure all small sails and prepare for the Hurricane of your lives!" Some of the crew gave their captain strange looks, but they again jumped to do as they were ordered without argument. Rielle joined Vesth and Strolm as the crew scurried about their work.

Several men began tying heavy ropes to the main mast and systematically began fastening the other ends around the waist's of the rest of the crew. The rest of the companions gathered around the Helm and waited quietly.

As each of them had a rope securely tied around their waist, the sailor Rielle had spoken to earlier returned and handed Rielle a small bundle of cloth. She nodded to the man and he hurried away to join the rest of the crew in preparing the ship. Rielle untangled the bundle and held it out to Nysisset.

"I believe this is what you were hoping for?" Nysisset's eyes glittered and she licked her lips hungrily as she slowly lifted the black-gemmed amulet to eye level.

"It is more beautiful than I had thought it would be." She whispered. She took the simple amulet and slipped the golden chain around her neck. Immediately she took in a sharp, shuddering breath, and her purple eyes darkened almost to the point they had been before she had left the Mercury Mountains. Her tattoo's grew around her eyes and they flowed as if they would come alive.

"The power is incredible." Nysisset gasped.

"Be careful to control it, Nysisset. It will only serve a master with a steady hand. It would be best not to use your powers until you have fully adjusted to it." Solidus spoke through Rielle with a tone that held a command more than a suggestion. Vesth noticed Strolm's eyebrows raise in surprise and stared down his old friend with a slight shake of his head. Strolm spared a glance back at Rielle before nodding to Vesth and turning back to focus on guiding the ship.

Nysisset looked at Rielle, an obvious struggle taking place in her expression before she nodded and her tattoo's slid back down to become the snakes on the sides of her neck once again.

"As you wish Master Solidus." Rielle nodded and her eyes returned to normal.

"Be careful, Captain Strolm, we are approaching the barrier that protects the island." Rielle said, turning to look forward again.

"I can see that." Strolm muttered uneasily. Many of the crew paused to look up and the frosty white barrier that shimmered as it rose from the sea.

"Who told you to stop working?" Strolm roared at his crew. "Get those lines secure before we pass that wall!" The men jumped with renewed energy and hurried to do anything they could find that might need done.

"So what makes you think we are going to have a storm missy?" Strolm asked, glancing back at Rielle over his broad shoulder. Rielle continued to stare forward, seemingly through the white barrier before them.

"Leviathan waits for us beyond the protection of the Temple of Alenon." Strolm's jaw dropped open.

"The Leviathan is waiting for us? Then what in blazes are we sailing out there for?" Strolm asked, letting one hand fall from the ship's wheel. Rielle glanced at him calmly.

"Because we have no other alternative. Besides, Lord Leviathan will listen when I speak to him. He will listen to reason, or I will drive him away by force. Your ship will be safe, Captain, as long as your men are ready to weather the storm that Lord Leviathan will bring with him." Strolm stared at Rielle for a moment before looking at Vesth. Vesth nodded and motioned to Strolm's hand.

"Best do as she says Strolm, I have seen her do many things beyond belief. Besides, I do not think this creature will leave until we have confronted it. We either face it or starve to death waiting here." Strolm's eyes narrowed as he once again took the wheel in both hands.

"The next time you decide to save my hide, remind me to kill you. This is not worth what I owed you." Vesth nodded.

"In any other time I would have agreed with you." Strolm shook himself angrily and turned back to his crew.

"Tie down everything that is not part of the hull! Get those sails set, and for glory's sake, SECURE THOSE LIFE-LINES!!" Strolm's crew whipped into a frenzy, rushing back and forth, scared more for what their Captain might do than for anything they could imagine they might be sailing into. Nysisset nodded with a satisfied grunt.

"You rule your crew with an iron fist Captain." Strolm didn't even spare Nysisset a glance.

"My men do what I say, or I beat them black and blue and leave them at the nearest port. They know it and do everything I order, even if they don't like it. It has saved our sorry hides more than once."

"We are crossing the barrier." Rielle stated quietly. Vesth expected them to crash against the white barrier, but it slipped quietly past without the slightest hint it had ever been there. Everyone stumbled as the ship lurched. The calm sea suddenly erupted violently around them, and heavy rain crashed down onto the ship.

"Seal the hatches, Bailers keep those buckets moving! I need men on the sail lines, keep 'em tight!" Strolm called over the roar of the ocean. He spun the wheel and turned the ship to catch the wind. The ship groaned and pulled against the wind, slicing through the water and crashing over the violent waves.

"We are going to get pulled into the center of the storm." Vesth yelled over the wind.

"Don't you think I already know that!?" Strolm roared back. "Just let me run my own blasted ship!" A wave washed over the side of the ship and everyone struggled to stay standing as the ship tipped sideways in the deluge.

"Keep those Life-lines tight! I don't need anyone gettin' washed overboard." Strolm cursed as several men struggled to secure the lines tied to the mast. They crashed into another wave and the main mast groaned under the stress.

"Ease up Strolm." Vesth yelled.

"What in blazes do you think I am doing!" Strolm yelled back. Strolm struggled with the wheel as another waved crashed against the side of the ship.

"Segine!" Vesth called and grabbed the wheel. Segine stumbled around to Strolm's other side and heaved against the wheel.

"Leviathan draws you to the center." Delgorin called loudly. "Turn straight into the eye or He will tear us apart." Strolm growled and Vesth growled right back.

"Just do it Strolm! We don't have any other choices here." Strolm grunted at Vesth before looking at Segine.

"Alright knight, I need you down with the crew. Haul the sail up and tie it down. No way we will make it across the wind like that with the sail down." Segine nodded once and struggled down onto the main deck, shouting at the crew to raise the sail. Strolm and Vesth continued to struggle with the wheel as the ship lurched and bucked. Marina and Delgorin held tightly to the railing while Nysisset and Rielle leaned on each other, fighting to stay standing.

Segine nudged two men out of the way and grabbed a line, heaving with all his strength against the rope. The sail inched its way up the mast until it was bunched up at the top.

"Tie it down. Make sure it doesn't get away from us." Segine yelled at the crew, who immediately started securing lines to posts along the rails.

"TIDAL WAVE!" A man yelled down from the crow's nest. Everyone looked up to see an enormous wave forming dangerously close to the ship.

"Everyone grab hold of something!" Strolm roared as he and Vesth struggled to turn the ship into the oncoming wall of water.

"Marina!" Rielle yelled as loudly as she could. Marina stood, Delgorin doing his best to steady her, and she placed her hands together. Purple energy flowed down her arms and into her hands as she concentrated her power as quickly as she could.

"Whatever you plan on doing, do it quickly." Vesth groaned, setting his shoulder against the wheel. Marina gasped as the tidal wave loomed over them.

"Not enough time." She quickly stepped forward and pushed what energy into her hands she could as she released it in a sharp wedge that slashed into the wave, breaking up the water over the ship. Marina grasped the rope around her waist with both hands as she fell back, and Delgorin wrapped an arm around her shoulders when he could reach her. The water crashed down on the ship, temporarily drowning everything and tearing at the ship and crew.

Strolm and Vesth were thrown back and the wheel spun uncontrollably. Many of the crew were nearly washed overboard and Segine, clinging to the sail line with one hand, grabbed a sailor as he slid past with his other. The wave passed, and the ship lurched to one side. Rielle threw herself at the wheel, trying to stop it's spinning, and successfully managed to bruise most of her ribs as the wheel's handles hit her. Vesth managed to stand and again threw his shoulder into the wheel, stopping it. Strolm was close behind, and the two men managed to straighten the ship.

"I see an empty Life-line." Strolm yelled, motioning with his head. "Who did we lose?" A single line ran from the mast, up to the helm, and over the rail.

"Nysisset!" Rielle screamed, clutching at her injured ribs as she tried to stand. Segine heard Rielle's scream and dropped the sailor in his hand and ran, as best he could, up to the helm and grabbed the life-line. He heaved at the line with all his strength and a broken end jumped over the rail and onto the deck.

"No!" Segine yelled, and before anyone could stop him, he had torn the line from around his own waist and jumped over the rail into the angry waters after Nysisset.

"Stupid Fool." Vesth swore as he and Strolm continued to struggle with the wheel.

"What next?" Strolm complained with a grunt.

"MAELSTROM!" Came the cry from the crow's nest. Strolm growled.

"I didn't mean I wanted more of this." Rielle stood calmly, her arms falling to her sides and Solidus spoke.

"It is the eye of the storm. Leviathan dwells at the center of the maelstrom."

"Great! We can invite him for tea and blasted biscuits!" Strolm swore again. Rielle nodded to Vesth.

"Steer into the maelstrom let it's current's carry the ship."

"And drag us to a watery grave." Strolm interjected.

"Leviathan will be dealt with before the ship is harmed any further." Solidus said, with a note of finality. Strolm growled angrily as he twisted the wheel and pointed the ship at the rushing waters that formed the edge of the maelstrom. Rielle walked calmly down onto the main deck and to the side of the ship that faced the center of the whirlpool. The ship steadied as it entered the smoothly spinning water of the maelstrom, and Rielle stood easily beside the rail.

"Lord Leviathan, I seek an audience." Solidus spoke in a quiet voice that carried across the water. A ripple emanated from the center of the whirlpool, followed by an extremely low rumble.

"Don't let your anger towards me affect you so. Let us speak civilly." Another ripple, more violent than the first, followed by a louder rumble. Solidus growled impatiently.

"Show yourself, Leviathan. It is not your place to treat me so." The anger in Solidus's voice struck the water with physical force, causing the ship to shake and shock-waves that traveled across the water's surface. A heavy silence filled the air for several seconds before the Maelstrom slowed nearly to a stand-still and the water at its center boiled angrily. An enormous draconic head broke the water's surface and glared angrily at Rielle on the ship.

"It is not my place? You have no right to command me,

Pravin Solidus. You push the boundaries of this world further than all those before you. You cannot break the laws of this world and expect to have any authority over me. The ocean still cries out in pain from what you did." Rielle stood tall and glared back at the creature.

"I am well aware of the pain I caused the world, and I have already paid dearly for what I did. I am, however, still working to bring this world into balance, and if you think that I will allow you to hinder me you are sadly mistaken." The crew on the ship stood and stared, unable to move from the weight of their awe. Marina and Delgorin stood and watched as Solidus spoke. The giant creature shook it's head with a growl.

"The sea cries out for recompense, It's pain is my pain. I will see you punished for your violation of the laws." When Solidus spoke, his voice carried a strength and authority that far out-weighed the anger that the creature in the sea radiated.

"The seas are the domain of Great Titan Perion, not you Leviathan. Upon this ship stand three of the four Alenon Guardians under the domain of their Patroness, not under your influence. There were also four companions on which hinges the balance of this world, two of which were washed away in your blind anger and another that acts as my host. Would you deny the Six and take your anger out on the sole individuals who can heal the scars of the world?" The rain slowed, and then stopped altogether. The maelstrom ceased to spin and the sea became calm.

"Why do you persist? Why do the Six let you free from a sin that would have been a death sentence to your predecessors? Why do you do so much to harm the world, yet try to save it in the same breath." As the sea, the creature's voice had become calm. Solidus sighed.

"I am free to do as I must, because there are no more to take my place if I were to pass. The world, and the balance, are all I work to protect. To set a broken bone, more pain must be caused. To set the world in balance, the world will endure pain and stress that may seem likely to break it. But the pain will pass, and when it does, the world will be stronger for it. You see the life of the waters, their ebb and flow, but you do not see the rest of the world as it is in balance." The creature remained silent for several long moments before speaking again.

"The Six still have faith in your wisdom, Silver Mage. That should have been enough for me from the beginning." Rielle nodded.

"So then, you will do what must be done?" The draconic head nodded in return.

"The seas will be calm for the rest of your voyage. And those that were lost will be under my protection." Rielle nodded again.

"Then we will be on our way. But, Leviathan, Do not let your emotions rule you. Lose yourself and strike at me again, and I will strike back. Remember, you helped the Six bind the elements together in balance, but you are Not required for them to remain in balance." The creature closed its eyes and bowed it's head, slipping back into the sea.

"I heed your words, Master Solidus. It will not happen again." Everything was silent as Rielle turned back to look at the crew.

"Captain Strolm, take control of your ship once again." She

turned and looked to the south, an arm rising to cradle her injured ribs. "We sail for the Mercury Mountains."

9

༄

Chapter Nine

The scent of salt and sand filled the air. A few gulls called not far away, and the sound of small waves flowing across the beach hung quietly in the air. Segine groaned, lifting his face from the sand and looking around with unfocused eyes, trying to see where he was.

As his eyes began to focus, he could see that he was on a wide beach with a thin forest rising up not too far away. As he looked around, he noticed a black haired figure lying a few feet away. Segine painfully raised himself up on his hands and knees and crawled to their side and rolled them over on their back.

"Nysisset." He spoke hoarsely, shaking her carefully by the shoulder. Nysisset moaned quietly, and her eyes fluttered open.

"What happened?" She asked, sitting up and putting her head in her hands. "I feel like my head is being crushed." Segine rolled into a sitting position.

"I am not sure. I remember being on the ship, trying to keep it in one piece, but after that everything is a blur."

"Where are we now? Do you recognize our surroundings?"

Nysisset remained hunched over with her head in her hands, obviously expecting Segine to do the work. Segine turned painfully, and once more examined his surroundings.

"There are trees not far from here, and I can see the mountains on the far horizon. Judging by the position of the sun and the type of trees, I would say we are on the far north-east coast of Hortaal." Nysisset groaned.

"I could have done without the explanation." She complained.

"I am sorry." Segine said, turning back to her. Another groan escaped her lips.

"I can do without your apologies too knight. You say we are on the north-east coast? Then Master Solidus must have succeeded in calming Lord Leviathan. Since we are not back on the ship, or drowned, Lord Leviathan must have brought us to shore." Segine tried to remember what had happened, but everything after he had jumped overboard was blank. After a few moments he shook his head and rose to his feet with a grunt.

"Well, we can't stay sitting here on the beach. It's too exposed, and we have nothing with us, either to shelter or hide ourselves. We should head for the trees and make a camp until we can find some food and fresh water." Nysisset sighed.

"Whatever will get you to stop talking. Help me stand." She held her hand out and Segine took it uncomfortably and carefully pulled her into a standing position. Nysisset wobbled as she stood, and nearly fell back down again.

"Are you well?" Segine asked, his second hand moving to steady her. Nysisset snatched her hand away from his and growled at his other hand.

"I am fine." Without waiting for him to speak again, she

gingerly made her way up the beach towards the forest. Segine's hands fell to his sides and he followed quietly behind her with a pained expression.

They slowly walked away from the beach and into the thin forest a short ways away. Nysisset led the way, inspecting each tree, and often clinging to them for support. Segine stood painfully by, wanting to help, but not daring to act as Nysisset scowled angrily at each tree she had to lean on that they passed. Eventually they came to a small clearing with a small pine standing at the far side.

"This will do." Nysisset grumbled. She investigated the pine and nodded after a few times walking around it and looking under the branches.

"We can sleep here. The tree should provide good cover and keep others from detecting us." Segine looked skeptically at the small pine.

"There isn't enough room under there for both of us." Nysisset harrumphed.

"Of course there is. There is more than enough room for two bodies to lie side by side beneath the branches. Then again," She eyed Segine's dented breastplate.

"I do insist you remove that uncomfortable thing if we are going to be sleeping together." Segine jumped back in shock.

"Sleeping together?! I think not miss, it is not proper. I will make a camp in the center of the clearing and start a fire. After which I will make two Separate places to sleep. Only white clouds pass overhead, and this is not the season for storms. We should not need shelter tonight." Nysisset sighed in exasperation.

"Fine, do things your way knight. I am too exhausted to

argue." Segine moved quickly, almost running to set up the camp. Nysisset lowered herself to the ground and set her back against a tree to rest.

Segine quickly built a small fire, placing it close enough to Nysisset for her to feel the warmth. He then laid several fallen pine branches in two distinct rectangles on either side of the fire and covered them with dead leaves. Once the beds were finished, he disappeared into the forest for several minutes before returning to the camp with a thin piece of bark filled with water. He knelt and held it out to Nysisset, who drank it thirstily.

"I found a shallow stream not far from here. The water should be enough to get us through the night." Nysisset took a breath after finishing the water and wiping her mouth.

"I really don't care where the water came from knight, just bring me more." Segine suppressed a sigh and nodded, quickly leaving the clearing again. Segine made several trips between the camp and the stream, providing Nysisset with the water she demanded. Upon returning the final time, he found Nysisset carefully lowering herself onto one of the beds. She excepted the water he brought and then laid back with a strained sigh. Segine set the bark aside and placed a few more sticks of wood on the fire.

"I will keep watch." Segine said, moving to stand.

"Don't be a fool." Nysisset growled angrily. Segine stopped halfway to his knees.

"You can't fool me, knight. You barely have the strength to stand, let alone go for any length of time without rest. What makes you think you can keep watch, or fight off anything that might enter the camp?" Segine kept his eyes slightly lower than

Nysisset's. His hand strayed to the sword that was somehow still securely tied to his hip.

"But we must set a watch, wild animals or thieves could..."

"Could what!" Nysisset cried in exasperation. "We have no food to interest any animals, and we have nothing worth stealing. As far as I can see, there is no reason there should be a watch. If you don't rest then you wont even be able to lift that sword to fight anyway. So lay on your 'bed' and sleep." Segine searched for an argument, but due to his own fatigue he was finding it hard to think clearly and eventually nodded, silently agreeing with Nysisset. He sat back down and poked at the fire.

"I will stay up and tend the fire a little while longer then, just to be safe." Nysisset harrumphed.

"Fine, but if I find out you tried to go off on some fool errand before you rest, then when I am done resting I will put you down in the dirt myself." Segine nodded hurriedly and busied himself with the fire, careful to avoid Nysisset's glare. After a few moments Nysisset turned her head away from the fire and closed her eyes to sleep.

Segine sighed and added a few more sticks to the fire. He sat quietly, watching the flames dance, often catching his eyes drifting towards Nysisset. He shook his head to clear it and tried to focus on the fire again. Slowly his eyes began to blur and he wobbled in place for a few moments before finally laying down to sleep.

The still, salty air was quiet, and the soft lapping of the water on the beach quickly lulled him to sleep. His last thoughts drifted away as he became dimly aware of another smell wafting into the camp as he slipped into dreams.

"pitch"

* * *

The south cliffs of the Mercury Mountains were shear and jagged, reaching like claws towards the sky. Rielle stood, hands resting on the rails of the ship, watching as the cliffs moved slowly by. The ship crept along sluggishly as the spotters fished in the water before the ship with long poles.

"There is a reason no one sails around the south end of Galbrea." Strolm complained, hands turning white as he tightly gripped the wheel.

"We will be fine as long as we don't move too quickly." Vesth stated calmly, though his armor creaked from the tension in his folded arms.

"We are almost there." Rielle said, not turning as she watched the cliffs. "Once we are there, Captain Strolm, you may turn your ship and leave this place."

"Where is there?" Strolm asked, his agitation plain. "There is nothing here but cliffs and jagged reefs for two hundred leagues."

"Nevermind where we are going. It is not for Mortals to know." Marina said snappishly. Strolm huffed and Delgorin chuckled nervously.

"Don't mind her young man, She is not in a pleasant mood."

"There." Rielle pointed at the cliffs.

"All Stop!" Strolm yelled. Men hoisted the sails up and an anchor was dropped. The spotters at the front of the ship set their poles against the nearby reefs and the ship drifted to a smooth stop.

"Do you see it Delgorin?" Rielle asked. Delgorin stepped to Rielle's side and shaded his eyes, scouring the cliffside.

"I believe I do." The old man disappeared and a few sailors

made the sign to ward away evil. The air was still for several moments and then Delgorin returned.

"The shelf is large enough for all of us to stand, but only just." Rielle nodded and turned to Strolm.

"Your service to us has been much appreciated Captain Strolm. You may return to your home or wherever you so choose. When we next meet we will discuss payment for your service." Strolm shook his head.

"If I never have to make such a voyage again, that will be payment enough for me." Strolm turned on Vesth and shook one finger at him. "But you and I are even now, Hear me? You should owe me twice what I owed you, but then I would probably have to make another life-ending trip to find you and make you pay up. We are even, And I don't want to hear anything about it again." Vesth nodded solemnly.

"We are even. But if you ever need a favor, you only have to ask." Strolm harrumphed and nodded.

"Should I be telling them?" Vesth shook his head.

"Give it some more time. If things get any worse then send the message." Strolm nodded and he and Vesth pounded their fists together. Vesth joined Rielle and Delgorin and they all looked at Marina. Marina stared back for several moments before sighing.

"You are sure this is the only way?" Rielle nodded once. Marina sighed again and then joined them.

"Be ready, this will take your breaths away." Delgorin told them, and they nodded their acknowledgment. A feeling like breathing ice stabbed at their lungs and light flooded their vision. A few seconds passed and they found themselves standing on a stone shelf high above the water. Miniature figures could be seen moving around on the small ship below as it began to slowly turn.

Delgorin gave everyone a few moments to catch their breaths before leading the way along the narrow path into the mountains. Everyone was silent as they walked, not daring to speak as they focused on keeping their feet on the path. They walked for hours, eventually heading into the mountains on a wider footpath that looked like it had not been used in centuries. Eventually Delgorin stopped and looked around at the jagged gray stone.

"I feel it." Marina nodded and took the lead, making her way around a bend and stopping as the path tipped downward into a shallow valley, at the center of which stood an enormous structure, It's worn stone falling apart, and large columns lay fallen on the ground. Marina stepped aside for the rest to see and waved her hand to encompass the entire valley.

"Welcome, to the Temple of Balance." Rielle's eyes turned silver and Solidus spoke.

"Let us hurry. Lord Khornal is already waiting for us and the others will arrive soon. They will want to spend as little time here as possible." Marina and Delgorin both nodded and they hurried down the path as fast as they could without running.

As they reached the bottom Marina stopped and grabbed Delgorin's hand. Delgorin turned and held his hand out to Rielle, who took the old man's hand carefully. Delgorin smiled and tightened his grip which was, to Rielle's surprise, quite strong. Marina nodded to Rielle and spoke.

"Take Vesth's hand as well. Once we start across the valley, do not lose him, no matter what happens." Rielle turned and looked at Vesth, hesitantly lifting her hand out to him. Vesth looked at her hand and then threw a questioning glance towards Marina. She nodded once again and he looked back at Rielle, slowly reaching out and taking her hand in his.

"I will not let go until we reach the temple." He swore solemnly. Rielle nodded silently and nervously tightened her grip on both of the hands she held. Marina turned back and stared over the calm short grass of the valley.

As if from some unseen signal Marina took off at a dead run, Delgorin close behind. Rielle was nearly pulled off her feet and only just barely managed to start running without falling. Vesth fared better, seeming to have already been prepared to run.

It only took a few seconds after they started before a horrific roar surrounded them. In a matter of moments they were surrounded by a powerful storm that tore at them, threatening to pull them apart. Bits and pieces of rock and earth cut at their hands and faces as the furious winds tattered their clothing.

Suddenly, the storm was replaced with a searing heat that pulled the moisture from their bodies in great drops which immediately turned to steam. Rielle's eyes teared and she squeezed them shut, blindly following Delgorin and praying that her foot did not find something to trip on.

Just as Rielle felt as if she would roast where she stood, the heat died away and the air became thick and difficult to breathe. The line slowed to a crawl, like they were trying to run underwater, and Rielle struggled to let go and swim to the surface so she could breathe. But neither man would let go of her hands, no matter how hard she struggled.

Then an unimaginable weight fell on them. Rielle felt her body tremble and she hoped that the weight would crush her and end the nightmare. She felt Vesth press up against her back and his empty hand slid under her arm to support her. Delgorin gently pulled her along and suddenly they stepped out into the light and the weight was lifted.

Rielle gasped for breath and fell to the ground and she felt Delgorin's hand slide out of her's.

"We made it." Rielle heard Marina's voice, but was too exhausted to try and look at her. "I guess you were right Brother, I offer my apologies." Rielle didn't even notice Solidus take control of her body.

"You have no need to apologize, Sister. It is alright to question when you feel you must. We all made it across the valley, so we can focus on what happens now that we have reached the temple safely."

"But I didn't make it." Rielle said, realizing what had happened. *"I would have stopped and died in that place if Delgorin and Vesth hadn't been here to pull me through."* Rielle felt Solidus smile warmly at her.

"Part of a person's strength is the strength they receive from others. They would not let you fall, even when you did not have the strength to stand on your own. You have no need to be upset over that. One can do only so much on their own." Rielle took a few breaths and then realized she was still holding on to Vesth's hand. She looked at it, color appearing in her cheeks, and then carefully looked up at Vesth,

"Are you alright?" He asked her. She stared blankly for a moment before nodding quickly and allowing him to help her stand before letting go of his hand.

"I am fine, thank you." Vesth nodded uncomfortably and turned away. Rielle followed his gaze and caught her first look at the temple. The building was smaller than she had thought it was, but it was perfect in every detail unlike what she had seen from the other side of the valley.

"It changed." She stated, clearly confused. Marina nodded.

"What you saw was what the temple wanted you to see. It wants to appear unimportant and without value to the outside world so it can protect itself. Sometimes blending into the cliffs, sometimes appearing as a boulder, but always to keep it's true nature hidden from the world." Rielle studied the structure before her more closely, noticing the temple was carved from simple, and unadorned, gray marble.

"But on the other side of the valley, before we came across, it still looked like a temple." Marina nodded.

"It could sense the presence of a Balance Mage. Something it has not felt in many, many years. It did not want such a person to pass by without entering." Vesth looked suspiciously at the large doors and the pillars that formed an archway before it.

"It was... Lonely?" He asked. Marina laughed lightly, and Delgorin grinned.

"To put it simply, yes." Rielle walked carefully to the door and placed one hand gently on the pillar beside it. The temple seemed to hum, and the temple door swung open quietly.

"*It has missed me.*" Solidus said in reminiscent tones. Then his voice seemed to echo far away. "*Do not worry my old friend, we will spend time together very soon.*" The temple's hum became excited and Rielle led the way inside. Vesth fell in beside Marina and spoke in a hushed voice as they followed Rielle through the small, yet well lit, halls.

"What have we come here for?" He asked. "Rielle has told me that we only need the altar here, and I should not worry, But what we passed through in the valley to get here was not something that was created to protect a simple altar." Marina nodded solemnly.

"This temple is one of seven. Each guards a seal used by the Six Deities to bind the elements together when the world was created." Vesth's step never faltered, but his expression fell momentarily before he spoke again.

"Why would we need to come to such a place? Why would mortals such as us need, or want, to be near such a vast power?" Marina looked at Vesth and studied his face carefully.

"If I tell you, would you swear to let it continue? If I explain what will happen here would you, Can you, swear to stand by and do nothing?" Vesth's eyes traveled to the back of Rielle's head and, for several steps, he simply studied her.

"Will she be in danger?" He asked, not taking his eyes away from Rielle. Marina nodded.

"Most assuredly. But bare in mind that I argued with Solidus for many hours against taking this course of action and he would not falter. Rielle has also sided with Solidus and agreed to do what she believes she must. But you have not answered my question. Even knowing she is in danger, will you swear not to intervene?" Vesth walked on in silence for a few more moments before nodding slowly.

"If she has decided she must, I will not tell her she cannot. But I will stand beside her and protect her as I have also sworn to do." Marina nodded and also turned her gaze to Rielle.

"They are going to attempt to heal Rielle, and remove Solidus from her mind." Vesth's eyes widened in surprise.

"Can such a thing truly be done?" Marina nodded.

"Yes, but a body must be constructed for Solidus to inhabit, and removing him from Rielle will be very dangerous. If she is not sufficiently healed before he is removed, her wound may again threaten her life. If Solidus is not completely removed from her mind before he is transferred to his new body, then there would be a battle between their souls for the power to rule both spirits. Whichever soul wins would have complete control over the essence of both, and the loser would simply fade away and cease to exist."

"But even if there was a battle there would still be a chance that Rielle could survive right?" Vesth glanced at Marina, but she shook her head.

"Rielle's spirit and potential are very strong, greater perhaps than most who have come before her, But..." Marina's features hardened. "But, Solidus is on a level that no one can possibly match. Only two before him were his equals, and I am only just old enough to remember them. The first two Balance Mages created by The Six, had the power to shape the world as they deemed necessary. Power of which even Solidus has only a fraction. But with all the ties to the balance of the world which dwell within Solidus's very soul, no other soul could ever hope to overtake him. Even the Patriarch, and Matriarch, who were the first of his kind, would never have the strength to break his spirit." Vesth frowned deeply, and Marina took notice.

"But you are thinking of the worst possible outcome. Remember, that is only If their minds cannot be completely separated. And the danger, though very real, is slim. The real danger will be whether or not Rielle's body and mind can remain unscathed from the weight of 'Their' presence. It will be 'They' who complete the ritual. And no soul, no matter how strong it may be, will hold its full strength in such a flow of magical energies." Vesth's eyes focused completely on Marina.

"Who are 'They'?" Marina looked straight ahead and quickened her step.

"'They' are the Six who shaped this world. The Six Deities of Galbrea." Vesth stopped in his tracks, utterly speechless, watching blankly as the others hurried away, feeling nothing, and hearing only the last words Marina had spoken echoing in his mind.

"The Six Deities of Galbrea."

10

Chapter Ten

Segine's head pounded ferociously, and the shaking of whatever he was laying on wasn't helping. A groan escaped his dry throat and he immediately heard a metallic clang that shot sharp pains into his head.

"Quiet in there plainsman." The voice was gruff, and obviously drunken. Segine felt an elbow jab into his side.

"What's the matter with you, are you trying to catch their attention?" He heard Nysisset whisper angrily. Segine tried to open his eyes and look around. His vision was blurry and he couldn't seem to focus on anything.

"Who's attention?" He asked groggily. He heard Nysisset grumble.

"We were captured while we slept. Then we were drugged to keep us asleep. Apparently my body fought off the toxin long before yours did, I have been awake for hours already." Segine tried to sit up and a hand in the middle of his back pressed him back down.

"What did I tell you about getting their attention?" Nysisset growled. "These drunken fools don't care what or who they have in their cages, they lash out at whatever catches their eye." Segine relented and lay still.

"So we are locked up then?" Nysisset grumbled again.

"I just said that didn't I? If you must know, we are all locked in large steel cages on wheels and we are all chained to the floor. Not to mention we are stripped down to basically nothing. So quit trying to get us killed and stay still and quiet." Segine again tried to look around.

"Where are we?" Segine whispered. He heard Nysisset hiss quietly in agitation.

"How am I supposed to know? I have lived my entire life in the Mercury Mountains. Besides, it is getting dark and there is no way to see landmarks anyway. So quit asking stupid questions and lie still." Segine relented and lay quietly, slowly becoming aware of the cold iron chains around his wrists and ankles.

The cages rolled on for what felt like little more than an hour before a halt was called. The cages were rolled into a large circle and the men driving them started a fire in the center, sitting around its warmth and leaving their captives to fend for themselves. Segine sat up, finally able to see, and looked at what little of the forest he could see around them.

"I think we are in the deep forests of Hortaal." He told Nysisset, who stared moodily at the men around the fire.

"Not yet to the Moon Witch forest, but close enough that the trees have not been logged. They have been given the chance to get very old."

"Ooh, fantastic. Now that I know that useless fact, my life is complete." Nysisset growled sarcastically. Segine frowned.

"When we escape we will need to know where we are so that we can get to safety." Nysisset tugged angrily at the chain attached to her right wrist.

"And how do you plan to escape? Even if you could get unchained somehow, your armor and sword are gone. How do you plan to get away without getting caught or killed?" Segine looked down at his hands in thought. Nysisset grunted.

"I thought so. At least we have a cage to ourselves so that I wont have to deal with more than one simpleton." Segine continued to stare at his hands, then he looked at the floor of the cage where the chain was fastened and pulled on it. He tested the chain a few times, tugging at it and feeling the weight of it in his hands, the wheels in his head slowly turning. Then he looked around to see if anyone was near and yanked up on the chain.

There was a sharp cracking sound from the floor and the bolts attached to the wood groaned in protest. Nysisset jumped slightly with surprise.

"Are you trying to warn the whole world that we are here?" She hissed, though she did spare a glance to reexamine the floor she sat on.

"I think I could pull our chains from the floor. The wooden floor should be weak enough to break and we could make a run for it." Nysisset paused a moment to consider the possibilities, and the possible arguments she could lobby against the knight, but she was beaten to it.

"I wouldn't try that if I were you." Nysisset's eyes widened, reflecting the moonlight like a feral cat's, and peered into the darkness.

"Who is there? And what do you want." A low, smooth

chuckle met her question and a large man with a long white scar trailing down the side of his face stepped out of the shadows.

"I am Tharis Lionsmane. And I already have what I want. I have you." Segine turned and strained against his chains, causing the floor to creak again.

"Tsk tsk tsk." The man waved his finger at Segine. "Breaking your chains free wont help you much. Even if you didn't attract the attention of the drunken fools who drive the caravans, there are still plenty of us who are sober. If you were to leave your cage, you would be shot on sight." As if to prove his point, an arrow hissed through the air and embedded itself in the floor of the cage, narrowly missing Segine's arm. The man reached into the cage and pulled the arrow out, looking at it without interest before throwing on the ground behind him.

"And my archers never miss. But I am willing to help you out." Nysisset's eyes narrowed and Segine loosened his grip on his chains.

"What is the catch?" Segine asked. The man grinned, stretching his scar and causing his smile to list to one side.

"You fight for me in the arena, and I will set you free. I can see you for what you are, knight. None of those drunken fools over there had any idea what we had found when we stumbled upon your little camp. But I do not like to let talent go to waste, so I took you for myself before they could throw you in with the rest of the fodder." Segine growled.

"You want me to participate in an illegal fight so you can gain profit. I will not debase My honor in such a way." The man moved so quickly that Segine and Nysisset had almost no time to react. He reached through the bars of the cage, grabbed Segine's chains in one hand, and smashed him against the bars.

"The Arena is just as much about honor, as it is money, Boy. I fought in the arena for years to earn enough honor to become a free man. In the arena my name is a legend. And if you want your freedom you must do the same. That or die by the hands of another." Segine growled.

"We do not have years to waste fighting senseless battles."

"Which is why you need my help." The man said, releasing his grip on Segine. "I can get you out of the arena much more quickly if you agree to fight for me." Segine's stare hardened. Nysisset quickly looked at the sky and then back at the man.

"Could you get us out by the next Darkmoon Cycle?" She asked. The man looked at her, sizing her up, before answering.

"You want out by the New Moon? That is only a few weeks away." Nysisset nodded.

"Two weeks, four days. Can it be done?" The man looked Segine up and down.

"If you have the stamina to fight multiple foes each and every night. Then I might just convince some of the higher bidders that it would be worth sponsoring your freedom. But you would have to make a name for yourself, and get the crowds on your side. Put on a good show and I might, Might, be able to get you freed by the New Moon." Nysisset glared at Segine and the knight finally relented.

"Fine, I will agree to fight for you, but with three conditions." The man's eyebrows raised questioningly.

"Conditions?" Segine nodded.

"First, the girl will be spared from the arena." Segine threw

Nysisset a stony glare to silence her protests. The man scratched his chin.

"She would have to be indentured to one of the patrons of the arena. She would have to wait on them, hand and foot, but she would be spared from the bloodshed, and would also be able to watch your fights." Segine nodded and silenced Nysisset with another look.

"That is good enough." The man folded his arms across his massive chest.

"What about your other conditions?" Segine held his hands up until his chains were tight.

"Secondly, I will fight only with my own sword and armor." The man nodded.

"I have your sword in my posession, I will have to find the scumbags that stripped you down to find your armor."

"Then do it." Segine stated emphatically. The man grunted.

"And what of your third condition?"

"Third," Segine met the man's eyes with his own.

"Why are you helping us?" The man seemed mildly surprised by the question.

"Why?" Segine nodded and waited for an answer. After a few moments of silence the man turned and started to walk away.

"Because I was once known as Sir Tharis Ironfelt." Segine's jaw grew slack and he sat speechlessly in the cage.

"Rest, We reach the Arena tomorrow and then your real trouble begins." Tharis disappeared into the night and Segine slumped against the cold bars. Nysisset watched the man go and then looked at Segine.

"Ironfelt?" Segine nodded.

"The Ironfelt's were cousins to the ruling king of Laytrow. They died out years ago because of the loss of all their heirs in tournaments and accidents."

"Apparently not all of them." Nysisset said looking back in the direction that Tharis had left.

"And what about the Darkmoon? Why try to get out by then?" Segine turned his head to look at Nysisset. Nysisset looked up at the moon and her eyes filled with an eerie light.

"Because on the night of the Darkmoon Cycle my power will peak. You earn our freedom with your strength by then, Knight, or I will break us free with mine." Segine studied Nysisset's face, not liking the thought of any power she might use to free them. Nysisset stared at the moon for a little longer and then turned back to look at Segine.

"What is wrong with you? Didn't you hear the old knight? Get some rest already. The poison they used on us will have tired you out and I want you to be ready to fight when we arrive tomorrow." Segine blinked in surprise.

"What about you?" Nysisset scoffed.

"I told you already that my body fought off the poison hours ago. I am not tired in the least. Besides," She turned and looked over her shoulder at the drunk men around the camp fire.

"I am not the one who has to fight, and I do not trust these imbeciles. We belong to Tharis Lionsmane and more than likely stand to make him a fair bit of money. I wouldn't put it past most, if not all, of his companions to try and tamper with his fighter to swing things in their favor. Probably already have bets going over victors." Segine nodded slowly.

"That sounds logical." Nysisset sighed.

"Of course it is. It was I who said it. Now go to sleep or I will take steps." Segine slid carefully farther away from Nysisset.

"What about you?" Nysisset grumbled.

"Again with the same stupid question? I told you I am not tired. I will stay awake and watch over the camp. I can always sleep during the ride tomorrow if necessary, though I doubt it."

"But I could also..."

"No." Nysisset interrupted Segine. "You will sleep tonight. Right now. You are our first option to get free and find Rielle and the others. If you don't get us out by the Darkmoon Cycle then I will, and there will be far more bloodshed." Segine sighed and nodded, looking for a place to rest comfortably. Nysisset watched the knight for a moment and then sighed again, stretching her legs out flat and scooting closer to Segine.

"Lay your head on my lap, knight." She told him. Segine looked at her questioningly, suddenly realizing they were both clothed with a few rags that only just prevented them from being indecent. Nysisset scowled.

"Just do it. I will force you if I have to. I wont have you interrupting my night with your tossing and turning." Segine's cheeks flushed, but he nodded uncomfortably and did as he was told. Nysisset nodded.

"Good, now sleep. I..." She paused for a moment and then spoke again, almost gently.

"I don't want you getting hurt tomorrow because you are not rested." Suddenly Segine did not feel quite so uncomfortable, and he closed his eyes and felt Nysisset's warmth.

"Very well then. Goodnight." Nysisset's voice softened as he drifted into sleep.

"Goodnight... Segine."

*　*　*

Rielle hurt everywhere. She felt like every part of her body had been badly bruised. She shifted carefully and felt soft fur beneath her. She reached up and felt a down pillow under her head and the warmth from a fire radiated from somewhere nearby.

Rielle opened her eyes and found herself in a small house, a fireplace filled with heated stones next to her bed. She pulled the covers away from her and then sat up gingerly as a mild pain spread down her back. She sat on the side of her bed, rubbing her neck and trying to soak in the warmth from the stones.

"It is good to see you are finally awake." Rielle froze at the sound of the familiar voice. Her hand slowly dropped to her side and she turned her head to look over her shoulder to see who had spoken.

"It wasn't nearly as bad as Marina thought it was going to be. But It was still a little rough." Solidus sat in a simple wooden chair beside a short table covered in books in one corner of the small house. He looked up from the book he had been studying and smiled at her.

"Come now, don't look so surprised. A young lady such as yourself should not go around with her mouth hanging open." Rielle snapped her mouth shut and then spoke.

"Master Solidus?" Her throat and mouth were dry and the words came out as little more than a whisper. Solidus chuckled.

"I am glad you still remember what I look like after so long." Rielle tried to clear her throat, unsuccessfully.

"So, we succeeded then?" Solidus nodded.

"Yes we did. Though your mortal wound was not healed as

much as we had wished, you will still be able to function without too much restriction. And the rest of the wound will heal by itself in time." Rielle nodded and looked around the rest of the room.

"Where is everyone else? Mistress Marina and Master Delgorin and,"

"Vesth?" Solidus finished for her. Rielle frowned and Solidus smiled again.

"Marina returned to Alenon temple to help Agamemnon where needed. Delgorin returned to his wandering, in disguise so he could gather information undetected by the ones who are hunting us. As for Vesth, well, He has hardly left your side since we left the Temple. He only just left a few minutes ago when you began to stir to find food and water for you." Solidus blinked and looked at the doorway.

"And here he comes now." Vesth pulled aside the curtain that acted as a door and stepped inside holding a tray with a small plate of food and a mug.

"You are awake." Vesth stated, and Rielle thought she heard relief in his voice. He made his way to her bedside and placed the tray on a stand next to her.

"Are you feeling well? Is there anything I can get for you?" Rielle smiled up at him.

"No, Thank you Vesth." Vesth nodded but took the mug from the tray and placed it in her hands.

"Here, drink. You sound like you need it." Rielle quickly pressed the mug to her lips and poured the cool liquid into her mouth and swallowed. She took a moment to let it soak in and then she sighed gratefully and handed the mug back to Vesth.

"Thank you again Vesth. Did you bring this here for me?" She asked, pointing to the food. Vesth nodded.

"Of course. I had assumed you would be hungry when you woke and I wanted to be prepared. If I was mistaken I apologize." Rielle smiled warmly.

"No need to apologize. Thank you for bringing it for me. I appreciate it." Vesth bowed.

"You don't need to thank me, miss Rielle. I will go and fetch you more water." With mug in hand, Vesth swept back out of the door and was gone.

"Go easy on the food." Solidus spoke from his corner, his eyes following lines of text in his book.

"It has been a few days since we left the temple and you have not eaten anything in that time. Your body will need to adjust to food again." Rielle nodded and carefully picked out something that she assumed was dry fruit and began to nibble at it.

"Where are we?" She asked as she ate. Solidus continued to read his book.

"We are in Bitreel. In a small village a short ways to the north-west of Tiasia's village." Rielle's chewing stopped and a tremble passed through her. Solidus closed his book and carefully sat it on the table and made his way to Rielle's bed. He sat next to her and put a comforting hand on her shoulder.

"There was nothing you could have done for Tiasia that you had not already done." Tears began to form in Rielle's eyes.

"It was my responsibility to protect her." Rielle choked, trying to prevent herself from crying. Solidus took hold of Rielle and cradled her head against his shoulder like a child.

"She is doing what she was born to do. And it is a very

important duty. You gave her what she needed to be able to perform that duty."

"I... did?" Rielle asked between quiet sobs. Solidus nodded.

"In reality Tiasia was a very sad and lonely child. She caused trouble in her own village because she wanted attention. She wanted guidance and love, but no one would give it to her. Until you came to ask for her to join you." Rielle rolled her head and looked up into Solidus's eyes. Solidus smiled sadly.

"When you asked her to go with you, and told her she was important, she started to feel something she never had before. Acceptance. As you traveled with her, you cared for her and taught her the things that no one in her village would. And when she came together with everyone else she could see a bond between all of you and she felt at home. Then she planted the seed of change in all of you. Both Vesth and Segine managed to loosen up a little and actually feel something instead of locking away all of their emotions. Nysisset was turned and began, for the first time in her life, to see something other than darkness. And you," Solidus smiled and looked down at Rielle.

"You could finally let go of the past." Rielle felt like lightning suddenly coursed through her and more tears welled up in her eyes.

"You finally opened up, just a little, and let others in. You didn't just lead a group to do what you thought needed done, You befriended them and they became just as much a part of your family as Morien has been." Rielle felt understanding dawning on her, as if she had opened her eyes for the first time and was seeing everything in the light instead of the shadows. Vesth entered the room with the mug and a small pitcher and immediately saw Rielle's tears.

"Are you all right?" He asked, obvious worry in his voice. Rielle stood shakily, with Solidus's help, and stumbled over to Vesth and threw her arms around him.

"I'm ok." She cried into his shoulder. Solidus stood and took the pitcher and mug from Vesth and placed them on the table. Solidus looked at Vesth and then made hugging motions with his arms when Vesth looked unsurely at Rielle. Vesth haltingly raised his arms and put them around Rielle, supporting her as she shook with sobs.

"Are you sure you are alright?" Vesth asked. Rielle nodded with a sniffle.

"I have just been a fool." She said, slowly gaining control of herself again. "I haven't given a second thought for what all of you have done to help me. I never asked any of you if you really wanted to do all of this. Not once did I ask for everyone's opinions, I just told you what to do and expected everything to happen like I asked. I was a spoiled, highborn, brat and I am so sorry I dragged you all into this mess." Vesth could sense she was going to start crying again so he pulled her closer and patted shoulder comfortingly.

"You don't need to be so hard on yourself. We all chose to follow you, with the exception of Nysisset maybe, And we all knew the kind of danger we would be facing. We followed you because we trusted your judgment, even if you did not." Rielle rested quietly against Vesth's shoulder, grateful for his support and unsure she would be able to stay standing without it.

"Are Nysisset and Segine really alright?" Solidus nodded.

"They are fine. But their path goes in a different direction than yours for now." Rielle turned, and Vesth supported her until she reached her bed and sat down.

"And where does our path go now?" Solidus smiled.

"For now? It goes to breakfast." As if to emphasize this point, both Solidus's and Rielle's stomachs growled. Solidus sighed.

"Oh, how I have missed eating. Make sure she doesn't eat too much Vesth. And then make sure she rests. You will both need your strength when you leave tomorrow. I am going to go look for my own breakfast." With this, and an elaborate bow, Solidus left the house. Vesth took the pitcher and poured some water into the mug and handed it to Rielle.

"Drink. Most of the food here is dried and you will need the water." Vesth stood and went to the corner and grabbed the chair Solidus had been sitting in, bringing it around to sit beside the table. Rielle gratefully drank the water and then inspected her plate of food.

"Thank you again for all of this." She told Vesth. Vesth cleared his throat uncomfortably and nodded.

"I couldn't just let you go hungry." Rielle smiled and picked up the piece of fruit she had tried to eat earlier.

"Then I guess it is time to eat."

11

Chapter Eleven

Segine could hear the roaring of the crowd outside the thick timber gate. He stood moodily in a long loincloth.

"I thought I made it clear that I would fight only with my personal sword and armor." He told Tharis. The old knight grumbled.

"I heard ya the first three times. You have to fight empty handed and with no protection for your first fight. Call it an initiation. You have to prove yourself worthy of the arena before you can fight on your own terms." Segine crossed his arms and looked at the old knight.

"And what if I am not seen as worthy?" Segine glanced back at the gate as he heard an agonized scream and a roar from the crowd.

"Then the crowd's bloodlust will be settled and you will be free of the arena much sooner than planned." Segine grumbled and the older knight slapped his hand across Segine's un-protected back.

"Just make sure you gain the crowd's favor. Just surviving

won't be enough. You have to show them that you can hold your own, that you can think on your feet. You have to appease the crowds and thrust fear into the hearts of your opponents. If you don't, then they will see you as a target. If the crowd only sees a survivor, then all they will want is that survivor's death. If you show them a fierce warrior, they will cheer for your success." Segine sighed and nodded his understanding.

"One more thing." Tharis said as the timber gate began to swing open. "This first battle will determine your name within the arena. You will enter as only Segine. When you leave, depending on what you do, the crowd will give you a title. Make sure it will strike fear into your enemies. You don't want a name like 'Segine the merciful'. Your enemies would fight you without fear, expecting you to show them mercy, and it would make your fight's that much harder. If, however, you manage to be called 'Segine the Destroyer'. Not one soul who fought against you would be able to fight with all their heart, because of what they fear you would do to them." Segine frowned.

"I will not torture men just to be feared." Tharis shoved Segine towards the now open gate.

"After this battle you could be the biggest pansy in the world and it wont matter. But if you want to be able to get out of here in the time frame you specified, you better make this fight so awe inspiring that no sane man who hears your name will be able to stand without trembling." Segine growled.

"Do it or you won't be free by the New Moon." Tharis growled right back. Segine saw, in his mind, an image of Nysisset standing, drenched in blood, over a pile of corpses. He could almost hear her voice.

"I warned you to get us out of here by now, but you were too weak." Segine shook his head.

"Pray you never meet me on the field of battle." Segine warned as he stepped out into the open dirt pit. The gate slammed shut behind him and he found himself standing under the night sky in a deep pit carved into the ground. Around the top of the pit were stands of people sitting, shouting at the tops of their lungs, demanding that another fight begin. At one end of the pit were several booths, obviously reserved for more wealthy viewers.

Segine immediately saw Nysisset standing next to a rotund man in the largest booth. She wore a black velvet dress, was holding a tray with a pitcher and a wine glass, and she fixed Segine with a glare that sent ice down his spine. Segine became vaguely aware of several other men standing in front of identical timber gates, all looking fearfully around the pit. A voice was announcing the name of each fighter and the one who owned them.

"And finally we have a well built man from the Plains of Laytrow, owned by the legendary Tharis Lionsmane, the formidable Segine." The crowd roared and Segine could tell that the man yelling out their names enjoyed it. Segine stood, stone faced, inspecting the other fighters. They all had fear plain on their faces.

"Farm hands, villagers, one of them might be a blacksmith. I am expected to fight these wretches?"

"Of course you are." Tharis said through the gate as the announcer continued to elaborate on what kind of battle the audience would be treated to.

"Most fighters in the arena are just picked up off the side of the road, or taken from camps while they sleep. But be wary of these 'wretches'. A man afraid for his life will fight tooth and claw to survive, and that is not an opponent easily beaten. Just remember to make it good, or you will be stuck here for a long time."

"Fighters step forward!" The audience roared in anticipation as the fighters stepped into the center of the pit.

"I am sorry for what I must do to you men." Segine stated, still stony faced as he came withing earshot of the other fighters.

"But I cannot lose this fight. May all your souls find peace in the heaven realm should you die this night."

"What is this? Is the big man a priest?" The announcer called out to the crowd. "Is Segine truly worried for these poor lost souls? Or perhaps he is some sort of dark cultist wishing to send these men to serve his deity. Only time will tell." Segine growled.

"How I will enjoy beating the life out of you if ever we meet." Segine muttered, and the two men closest to him stepped back fearfully.

"Fight!" The announcer screamed and the fighters all charged one another in a fevered frenzy. Segine felt a burning anger growing inside of him. His fists clenched and his muscles bulged up his arms and across his powerful shoulders.

"I will never forgive them." He mumbled to himself. The closest man to him charged, screaming in horror and flailing his arms, trying to hit the big knight. Segine waited until he got close and then reached out and took hold of the man's flailing arms in one hand and lifted him off the ground. The man struggled, a look of terror in his eyes.

"I cannot let my self be defeated by such a pathetic excuse for humanity. A battle should be fought with honor." Segine balled his empty hand, and felled the man with one blow to the chest, knocking him across the pit to land, unconscious, in the dirt. The other men froze, terrified by the big man's strength. Segine growled.

"Have you no honor? No Pride!? I Will Not lose to scum like you." Segine charged them with a battle roar and knocked them all to the floor with a massive swing of his arm. Any man who got back up was immediately leveled again with another blow from Segine's powerful fists. In a matter of moments all was still and the crowd roared, jumping to their feet in their excitement. Segine heard the announcer call over the crowds roars.

"Incredible, sensational. None other than Tharis Lionsmane could have created such a fighter. The only question that remains is what to call him." Names and titles were shouted out at random by the people in the stands.

"No, no. Not quite." The announcer was saying. "None of these quite fit, can no one think of a fitting name?" Then Segine heard a clear shout from the direction of the rich booths. Segine whipped around to see Nyssiset leaning out over her balcony and staring down the man and shouting out a horrifying name.

"Magnificent!" The announcer yelled. "Truly capturing the essence of this magnificent fighter. The man who wished well their souls, and then struck them down without mercy. Like the Reaper himself. From this moment forward, in this arena, this man will be known as... Soul Reaper Segine!" The crowd's cheer was deafening, and Segine ceased to think as he was led away by a servant and back through the timber gate.

Once inside he was sat down and food and drink was placed before him. Segine ate mechanically, staring blankly at his plate until someone sat in front of him.

"You are blasted lucky, you know that." Tharis told him. Segine scowled. Tharis glared right back. "With all that talk of souls at peace, and honor and pride, I half expected you to get some half baked name that only just barely manages to identify you. That girl companion of yours might well have just saved your life." Segine grumbled and ignored his food.

"How is being considered a symbol of death save my life in any way?" Tharis's blow came hard and fast, catching Segine unaware across the face.

"You fool. She gave you the best title you could possibly have hoped for. With a name like Soul Reaper, what man would ever want to face you. Any small fish will get scared away outright, and any bigger fights you catch will raise your prestige tremendously. If you play your name right, it is possible you could actually reach your goal of getting out of here." Segine shook his head.

"There is no honor in fights like those. And even less if it is only a misguided name that prevents an enemy from fighting me." Tharis thumped his heavy fist down on the table.

"Of course there isn't. This is an illegal underground arena. People are kidnapped and forced to fight here. The only honor you will find here are the fights you will get when you have truly established your name. You want an honorable opponent? Then you have to work for it." Segine harrumphed and glared at his food. A servant whispered something to Tharis, who nodded and sent them away.

"Your lady friend is here to see you. When you are done talking the servants will escort you to your room. Since you both belong to me, you will share a single room here in the arena. When you are not fighting and she is not serving the VIP's that is." Tharis watched Segine for several moments, a fact Segine chose to ignore, then turned and left.

Segine sat quietly by himself until he noticed Nysisset practically glide into the room. She wore a sleek black velvet dress, slit up the side almost to her hip and cut low in the front. She walked comfortably over to the table and sat down across from Segine. Nysisset sat silently while he kept his face turned away, and eventually she sighed and grabbed something from Segine's plate and began munching on it.

"Why?" Segine asked, not looking at her.

"Hmm?" Nysisset didn't even bother to form a word around the food in her mouth.

"Why did you give me such a name?" Nysisset scoffed and swallowed.

"We are trying to get out of here as quickly as possible. A good name will help us do that. We have to rejoin with Rielle, Vesth, and Master Solidus, or did you forget?" Segine frowned and Nysisset growled. She reached out and grabbed him by the chin, turning his face and forcing him to look at her.

"You may not like it, but this is our reality. We are stuck here, and you have to fight whether you like it or not. You better get used to it. The sooner you get serious about getting us out of here, the sooner we can be on our way. Or have you decided to wait and let me do all the fighting?" Another image of Nysisset standing on a mountain of mangled corpses flashed in Segine's mind and he turned his head away again.

"I didn't think so." She said looking down at his plate again. "You better eat everything they gave you. I want you in as good of shape as you can be in. I don't want to watch you get hurt and jeered at for the amusement of those insects outside." Nysisset shot an icy glance at the gate into the arena. Segine risked a sidelong glance at Nysisset. She sniffed and looked back at him.

"Well?" She asked. Segine looked down at his plate and decided she was right, slowly picking through what was on his plate. While he ate, Nysisset entertained him with the story of how much she despised serving fat, rich, and snobby humans. Going into great detail on how much she would have liked to put a knife in the back of each of them didn't really help Segine stomach his food any more quickly.

Once he was done the servants entered the room and took his plate before asking them to stand and follow. They were taken to a long stone building and led down a short flight of stairs before finding themselves at a room at the end of the hall where Tharis stood waiting for them.

"This will be your room from now on. When you are not training or fighting, you will be here. Don't worry about not being shackled either. If either of you are seen outside of this hall without an escort you will be shot, no questions asked. Now, I suggest you get some rest. The arena fights are late at night so that the more wealthy patrons can get away from their duties to attend. However, you will still be expected to wake before noon to train. You train with me and my other fighters, fortunately for you there are only two others and I don't intend to lose my prize fighters by letting them kill each other." Segine grumbled and entered their room.

"Wait inside for me, knight." Nysisset told him. "I have something to discuss with our 'Master'." She obviously found it amusing to call Tharis their Master. Segine just shrugged and closed the door and looked around. The room was spars. There was no furniture of any kind, the walls were all solid stone, and the room was dimly lit by a small hole in the ceiling at the far end of the room. To one side of the room there was a thin pile of straw covered by some stiff linen. Segine assumed it must be what would pass for his bed during his stay.

At the other end was a shallow basin, carved from the wall itself, and filled with water. Segine walked over and inspected it. The water itself was passably clean, and the basin was close to the floor. Segine looked at his filthy arms and sat down to bathe himself. Just as he was finishing Nysisset entered the room, wearing a plain brown tunic and carrying a small bundle.

"Oh good. I was almost afraid you wouldn't have the sense to bathe yourself without being told." Segine grunted.

"I am a knight, I was raised to keep myself clean and presentable."

"Yes, of course you were." Nysisset responded sarcastically. She reached into her small bundle and pulled out a towel and threw it to Segine, successfully landing it on his head.

"Dry yourself and then come and sit with me." Segine looked questioningly over his shoulder, but Nysisset ignored him and sat down at one end of the bed. The towel was sadly insufficient to dry all of him, so Segine settled for drying his face, neck, shoulders, and arms before setting it aside and walking over to the bed. He sat down, being sure to keep a respectable distance between himself and Nysisset. Nysisset looked at him and then pulled a large shirt out of her bundle and held it out.

"You might as well put something on. You will probably get ill sitting down here with nothing but a piece of cloth tied around your waist. And I don't want to deal with the shame if you die down here instead of out there fighting." She waved her hand at the door. Segine gratefully pulled the shirt over his head and found that, for the most part, it fit. Nysisset unrolled the rest of her bundle to reveal it was a thin blanket, and at the center of the roll was a short knife. Segine looked at it in surprise.

"Where did you get that?" Nysisset sniffed haughtily.

"From Tharis, of course. Where do you think I would have gotten it?" Segine was clearly confused.

"But why would he let you have something like that?" Nysisset picked up the small knife in both hands.

"Because he knows why I asked him for it. And he knows I wont try and escape with it. Of course, his condition is that I leave it in this room at all times, which suits my purpose just fine." Segine did not like where this discussion was going.

"And what purpose do you plan for a weapon in our own room?" Nysisset shrugged.

"To kill assassins with it of course." Segine's eyes opened wide and he couldn't form his thoughts into words. Nysisset slammed the knife back down onto her lap.

"Oh don't look so surprised. I told you that this sort of thing would happen. Competitors try to kill off each-others fighters all the time. The best time for them to do that is while the fighters are sleeping. So I will do just the same as we did in our cage on the way here. I will stay awake and watch you at night so that no one can sneak in and kill you. Then I can sleep during the day while you are training and be able to wake up in time for the fights at night." Segine shook his head to clear it.

"I can't have you do something like that. You need sleep too, and I am sure Tharis posts guards."

"Guards can be bought." Nysisset interrupted him. "And I already told you that I will sleep during the day. I am a creature of the night and darkness after all." Segine saw the flicker of a shadow cross Nysisset's eyes and he blinked, unsure if he had actually seen anything there.

"But you would be in danger sleeping here by yourself, as well as if someone got in here with the intent of attacking us." Nysisset scoffed.

"I assure you, Knight," She held up her knife again. "I cannot use my full powers yet, but even with nothing else but this knife I am still more than dangerous enough to take anyone they could afford to send after us." Segine felt a lump grow in his throat. Nysisset stared him down for a moment then set her knife aside and placed her back against the wall, stretching her pale legs out before her.

"Now that we have settled that matter, I suggest you get some sleep." Segine blinked, not quite comprehending. Nysisset gave an aggravated sigh. "Lay your head on my lap, knight. Unless you can see something else around to use as a pillow. And don't argue with me. I want you in peak fighting condition. You can't do that by sleeping with your head on cold stone." Segine debated with himself internally before realizing that refusing Nysisset was simply not possible, nor intelligent.

He carefully stretched out and rested his head on her lap, closing his eyes and hoping that the dim lighting would prevent her from seeing his cheeks burn red. Then he felt her throw the thin blanket over him before shifting to lean against the wall more comfortably.

"You did well today." She spoke softly. Segine felt his embarrassment replaced with frustration.

"I did nothing of the sort." He told her, squeezing his eyes shut tighter. "Fighting poor wretches like that, who have been stolen from their homes, people with no fighting experience or skill. I was taught better, I acted shamefully in a moment of anger." He heard Nysisset sigh again, but her voice was still soft when she spoke to him.

"You had no other choice but to fight. And even though you could find no honor in such a fight, no reason to act out, you still managed to find the strength to fight against your principals and do what needed to be done. I cannot think of any fight more difficult than one you must wage within yourself." Segine opened his eyes and saw Nysisset watching the door passively. She spared him a glance and spoke again.

"Not everything in this world is fair or honorable. We must sometimes do things we would rather not, because they are the things we must do regardless of our principals. I think winning that internal struggle, and being able to do what must be done, is a battle well fought." Segine watched Nysisset's eyes soften and then look back at the door.

"Now sleep. I won't tell you nicely again." Segine closed his eyes and tried to clear his head and prepare for sleep. Then he felt Nysisset slowly start to stroke his hair, and she quietly sang a peaceful melody with words he did not understand. Slowly he felt his eyes grow sandy, and his thoughts more sluggish. Then he felt as if he were enveloped in a dense fog and soon he slipped into deep sleep.

12

Chapter Twelve

Rielle woke, her dream fading quickly as her head left her pillow.

"What did you see?" Solidus asked, his eyes never pausing as they glided quickly over the words of his book.

"I was holding a sword with a silver blade. I was fighting with it, but I did not have an opponent." Solidus looked up from his book.

"Practicing perhaps? Do you remember how you were holding this sword?" Rielle closed her eyes and tried to remember, but the images slipped away and she simply had to shake her head. Solidus nodded once and returned to reading his book.

"That is ok. You were not meant to remember just yet, it will come back to you in time." Rielle blinked.

"Not meant to... remember?" Solidus sighed and closed his book, setting it on the small table beside him.

"You hold a great deal of knowledge within you. Knowledge you will gradually gain access to as you need it." Rielle stared blankly at Solidus, not comprehending. Solidus scratched his chin in thought.

"Hmm. It is a difficult subject to speak of, at least without swaying your path." Solidus continued to scratch his chin thoughtfully. Rielle sat quietly, recognizing the silence as Solidus's way of ordering his thoughts.

"You are an old soul." Solidus finally told her, his hand falling to his side.

"An old soul?" Rielle couldn't imagine herself as any older than she was. Solidus nodded.

"Yes. When your soul was created by the Six, it was not immediately placed in a physical body and placed in the world." Rielle thought for a few seconds.

"So when I was created I was not immediately born? Is that how it works?" Solidus nodded, leaning back in his chair with his arms folded and closing his eyes.

"When the Six create souls they immediately place them within a body, an infant as yet unborn. The soul loses any prior knowledge of where they were before entering their body, and their experiences make them grow stronger and capable of living in the heaven realm. However, sometimes a soul that is created is destined for great things. Such as in your case." Rielle felt a small chill travel down her spine.

"I was destined for something great?" Solidus smiled.

"Do you not think what you are doing now is something great?" Rielle considered this.

"I guess I never really thought about it that way. I was just doing what I thought was the right thing to do." Solidus nodded.

"That is partially because your soul is already prepared to do what you are meant to do. It feels familiar, the right thing to do, as you put it. When the Six sense that a soul is destined for a greater purpose, it is kept with them for a time, instead of immediately being born. The Six want to prepare their children for their journey, so that they can be successful. You were raised and taught in the heaven realm before being born, so that you would have everything you needed to succeed." Rielle frowned in thought.

"But doesn't that defeat the purpose of experiencing life so that we can live in the heaven realm?" Solidus opened his eyes, glowing silver light filling their endless depths.

"You are very sharp. You make me proud as your teacher." Rielle felt herself blush and she quickly coughed to hide it. "Yes, you are correct in assuming that it would defeat the purpose of experiencing life. But do you remember anything from before you were born." Rielle shook her head.

"Of course not. How could you remember anything if you weren't..." She paused, realizing what Solidus meant. Solidus nodded again.

"Anything you knew before your birth was erased before you came into this world. All that is left is what your soul remembers by instinct. It feels something familiar and accepts it as memory."

"Like muscle memory?" Rielle asked. Solidus smiled again.

"Exactly. Your soul senses that it already knows something and quickly remembers how to do it. Which is why you have been learning to control your magic so quickly." Rielle looked down at her hands.

"I already know magic before I learn it?" Solidus chuckled.

"Some, yes. Take when you first learned to feel your magic flowing through you." Rielle thought back to her first experience learning from Solidus in the peaks of the Mercury mountains.

"I learned to put up a shield." Solidus nodded.

"Yes you felt the pulse of your inner power almost immediately, and it didn't take more than a few moments for you to figure out how to raise your shield. I have known mages who studied for months to do the same thing you did in a few minutes." Rielle felt shocked. Solidus nodded.

"Now you see. But don't let all of this go to your head. It is still going to be difficult for you to learn everything you need to know before the end of your journey. Remember when you tried to learn to create a ball of light?" Rielle nodded.

"I couldn't do it at all for a long time until I had no other choice." Solidus nodded.

"It was likely something you didn't learn before you were born. Or something you learned, but did not practice. Therefore it was harder for you to learn how to control it. I just want you to remember that everything will not just be handed to you on a silver platter. You still have to learn and grow like everyone else." Rielle nodded, and suddenly found herself lost in the light of Solidus's eyes.

"What about you?" Solidus smiled, letting Rielle stare into his eyes for a few more moments before closing his eyes and taking the book off of the table again. Rielle blinked, realizing she had been staring and quickly turned away.

"I was not destined to be great." Rielle couldn't believe that.

"How is what you are doing not great?" She asked him, finding a steaming pot on the table beside her bed and hurriedly poured herself some tea. She could feel Solidus smile behind her.

"What have I done that was great? I have pointed you in the direction you must go. Guided your actions, taught you to use your own power. It is you and your companions that have the potential to bring change to this world. I may only protect it as it already is. Now, I think that is enough discussion for today. You and Vesth must leave today if you want to reach your destination in time." Rielle sipped at her tea.

"The Temple of Wind? I know you said it was important for me to go there, but why?" Solidus sighed.

"So curious." Rielle felt the silence brought by Solidus thinking again.

"For the most part you will learn what you will be doing once you have been through the temple. For now, all you need to know is that you are not yet strong enough to finish this fight. You do not know everything you will need to know. You can gain what you lack by going through the temples that house seals. By entering the Temple of Balance you opened a potential that can only be filled by entering the other six temples."

"And the first is the Temple of Wind." Rielle sat her tea back on the table. Solidus nodded.

"The order is important. This is something that must be done in balance in order for it to succeed."

"Is there any other way?" Rielle jerked at the sound of Vesth's voice. Vesth stood in the doorway, holding two packs obviously filled to bursting. Solidus didn't react to Vesth's sudden appearance, and his eyes continued to glide over the words in his book.

"There are other ways." Solidus answered. "But visiting the Temples is the simplest. It is also one with a high chance of success. Of course, if you feel you truly do not wish to follow this path, I can give you another." Solidus's gaze momentarily left his book and fell on Vesth. Vesth shuddered as he felt like Solidus's eyes could pierce through him and see everything that he did not want anyone else to see.

"No. If you think this path is the best to follow, then I am not one to argue. I am only here to fulfill my duty to protect Rielle, and I will do so until my dying breath." Rielle felt herself blush, but also a painful stab in her chest as Vesth mentioned duty. Solidus was once again reading his book, turning the pages frequently.

"That is good. Now, did you have something to say?" Vesth blinked, remembering the reason for his entrance.

"Miss Rielle, The village elder expressed his wish to speak with you before we leave." Rielle nodded and stood, straightening her tunic and slipping her feet into a pair of soft leather shoes.

"Then I will go and speak with him immediately. We should be leaving as soon as possible." Vesth bowed and stepped aside as Rielle left the small room. Vesth placed both packs on the end of the bed and made his way to the small table where she had left the freshly brewed tea.

"Who placed your seal?" Solidus asked quietly. Vesth felt like a bolt of lightning had shot through his gut. He slowly turned to face Solidus, who was still skimming over his book, for which Vesth was grateful.

"It has been there since I was very young." Solidus carefully closed his book and stood.

"But you remember everything that happened to you?" Another bolt of lightning, and a lump forming in Vesth's throat as he tried to suppress the painful memories.

"I would not say I remember exactly." Solidus made his way around the bed to stand before Vesth.

"But it is why you were so adamantly against magic for most of your life. And why you joined..." Solidus trailed off and let Vesth struggle inwardly.

"I joined the Brotherhood because they saved my life. They were the only ones I had ever seen with the sort of strength they possessed."

"Capable of fighting against magic users?" Solidus smiled knowingly. Vesth squinted his eyes shut and nodded, And Solidus spoke again.

"But they are neutral, careful to maintain the balance as best as they can. You have been in contact with them several times since meeting Rielle correct?" Vesth nodded again.

"And what do they have to say about your current situation?" Vesth watched Solidus's eyes travel down to a pouch tied to his belt. Vesth protectively placed a hand over the pouch.

"They want me to watch." Solidus nodded.

"They don't know which side they should be fighting against and want more information." Solidus stated. Vesth nodded again.

"They can see the threat that is Borsa, but they have been given reports of your deeds and seem to think that you could also be an equal threat." Solidus chuckled and Vesth looked at the Hermit in surprise. Solidus held out his book to Vesth.

"Send this to the head of your order. Let him study it until the next time you communicate with him. I think he will find it a most interesting manuscript." Vesth took the book. It was small and ordinary looking, but it was obviously very old.

"Let them read this book. Then have them give it to the King of Gentry. I am sure he would be most grateful to have it in his library. Now," Solidus held out a hand and placed it on Vesth's chest. A burning pain seared through Vesth, making his veins feel as if fire flowed through them. Vesth struggled to breath, to yell, to cry, to do anything, but he was paralyzed at Solidus's touch. For several seconds Vesth stood, trying to endure the pain, and then it was over and he collapsed onto the bed. He hunched over, grasping at his chest with one hand and panting as sweat ran down his head and neck.

"I have reshaped your seal." Solidus told him, returning to his chair, where he picked up another book and began to read.

"You will find that you will have some slight increase in your strength and dexterity as your old seal was obstructing the flow of your first gate." Vesth took his time to get his body and breathing back under control.

"Why?" Solidus shrugged.

"If you want to protect Rielle, you will need to be calm and collected, and you will need to be at your best. Your old seal was unstable and I am sure you have had your share of problems with it in the past." Vesth clenched his fists, fighting down more painful memories.

"I have healed the damage they did when they forced your gates open. It will be far less painful for you to move now." Vesth looked over his shoulder at Solidus. At every turn the Hermit was an enigma to him. Each of his actions seemed random and disconnected.

"However," Vesth flinched as Solidus looked up from his

book. "I would suggest you do not use your key, as you have not trained your body to withstand the force that would be opened to you." Vesth felt his hand tighten over the pouch at his waist.

"You would gain a great deal of power even from opening the second gate. But you would exhaust yourself in only a few minutes, and opening the third would likely kill you." Vesth gave up his internal fight.

"If I must die to protect Rielle, then I will." A book struck Vesth squarely between the shoulder blades. Vesth jerked and turned back to see Solidus selecting another book to read.

"And how, exactly would that help young Rielle?" Vesth couldn't make his mouth work. "Do you honestly think that throwing your life away will help her, or make her happy even in the slightest?" Vesth turned away, unable to look at the Hermit even though he wasn't looking back.

"Rielle is strong, but she is a sensitive child. She would rather die herself than be forced to watch one of her friends die. Don't you remember how the death of Tiasia affected her." Vesth felt a pang in his chest at the mention of the little girl's name.

"I am not trying to scold you like a child." Solidus said softly. "But you must understand that your life is just as important to her as her own. Fight, protect her, grow stronger along with her, but know when you must retreat and survive. You are all important to the Balance. You all have a part to play. It is time you start to think of something besides duty. Something that is more important and will give you a greater strength when you fight for it." Vesth bowed his head.

"All I have is my duty." He said, but even he sensed that he could not speak with the same conviction he once had.

* * *

"So what did Solidus tell you before we left?" Vesth asked. "Why is he not coming with us?" Rielle shrugged.

"I don't know. He said that there was something else he had to attend to and that we could manage on our own without him for a while." Vesth nodded and looked down at the small chart in his hands.

"Well according to the map the Elder gave you, we really are not far from the Temple of Wind. A days journey, two at most." Rielle nodded.

"I think we should take things slowly for now. From what Solidus told me, the Temple of Wind itself is not particularly dangerous, but it has been abandoned since before the Age of Peace. There is no telling what could have grown inside it while it has been empty. I would like to spend some time practicing my magic and sword skills before we enter. I don't have Solidus with me to protect me anymore, I want to make sure I am ready to be on my own." Vesth nodded.

"I understand, but remember, you are not completely alone. I am here to protect you or, at the very least, guard your back." Rielle blushed slightly and nodded.

"Thank you. I am grateful to have your support." They walked along in silence for most of the rest of the day, stopping shortly before dark to set up a small camp.

They ate and Vesth instructed Rielle on using her sword until the darkness forced them to return to their fire. Rielle practiced controlling the fire itself. Making it rise and fall, and pulling out bits of flame to dance in her hand before dropping it back into the fire.

Vesth watched on passively, being careful not to show any emotion on his face. He was surprised at how far Rielle had progressed in such a short time since they had met. Her strength as a magic user had been almost non-existent and she had never held a sword in her life. Now she was using magic with ease, and Vesth was sure she could hold her own in a fight against a regular swordsman.

She was by no means a master at either, Vesth noted that Rielle quickly dropped a small flame as she let it get too close to her hand and almost burned herself, But Vesth was sure that she would be very soon if she kept progressing as quickly as she was.

"It just occurred to me that Solidus left the bundle that Mistress Marina gave you at the Temple in Laytrow." Rielle looked at the bundle beside her, a little fearfully.

"He told me that I might need it, but said I should not use it unless it was truly a matter of life and death." Vesth looked at the bundle.

"Do you know what it is?" Rielle nodded.

"Of course. Solidus called it 'Patriarch'." Vesth flashed back to his conversation with Marina in the Temple of Balance. Vesth looked at the bundle with a suspicious eye. Rielle took the bundle, untied the cords from around it and slid out a beautiful curved sword and scabbard, similar to Solidus's sword.

"Mistress Marina spent several hundred years forging it, but beyond that I know next to nothing about it. Solidus said I would learn in time, but that I should not draw him fully from his scabbard until I need him." Vesth flashed back again as Rielle referred to the sword as 'him'. Rielle noticed Vesth examining the sword and she held it out to him. Vesth simply stared at it.

"Its ok for you to hold him. As long as you do not fully draw the blade." She nodded a few times, holding it out for him to take it. Vesth carefully took the sword and held it in both hands.

It was light, and the balance was superior to anything he had ever seen before. The scabbard itself was a hard wood with steel folded over the top appearing to have a grain much like the lighter wood beneath it must have.

"If it came to simply defending yourself, this scabbard would be just as effective as the sword itself." He stated. Rielle nodded, watching Vesth closely as he ran an expert eye over everything. Vesth grasped the handle with one hand and looked up at Rielle. Realizing what he wanted to do, Rielle nodded and even leaned forward slightly in anticipation.

Vesth placed his thumb against the guard and carefully pulled the blade from the scabbard a fraction of an inch. The blade was crafted of shining steel, blackened Iron, blue and straw colored metals and veins of brilliant silver flowed across its surface like lightning. After a moment Vesth suddenly felt whispers start in the back of his mind, urging him to draw the blade and use it. Vesth quickly slammed the sword back into its scabbard and held it back to Rielle, making the sign to ward off evil as he did so. Rielle carefully took the sword back and locked eyes with Vesth, waiting to hear what he had to say. Vesth sighed.

"Mistress Marina is truly a master blacksmith. I have never held a sword of such perfect craftsmanship. But," Rielle inched her way forward, leaning towards Vesth.

"But?" Vesth sighed and looked down at the sword in Rielle's hands.

"There is something corrupt about that sword. I don't know what it is, but when I pulled the sword from the scabbard to look at the blade, I felt something inside me, telling me to draw the blade and use it on anything around me." Rielle stopped inching forward and looked down at the sword in her hands.

"I think that, unless I spent a great deal of time to prepare, I would be overwhelmed by that voice and be unable to control myself." Vesth looked at the sword and then up to Rielle.

"I would be very careful with that sword." He told her. "It is a blade breaker. A perfect sword capable of overcoming any other it clashes with. I know you have an unwavering will-power, but please be careful. Even you might be over taken by it if you are not prepared to use it." Rielle's features hardened and she nodded. She slipped it back into it's cloth bundle and retied the cords around it.

"I will only use this sword if no other option is available." Rielle said, setting the bundle aside and picking up the sword that Solidus had found for her to use in place of his.

"This sword is good enough for me. If it breaks, I can always use my power to protect myself. Only if all else fails will I use the Patriarch." Vesth still felt chills at the mention of the sword's name. He felt like it should have some significance, but he didn't know what it could be. He shook his head, dismissing the idea as insignificant.

"I suggest we get some rest." He said, standing and moving

towards the edge of the camp. "I will take the first watch." Rielle nodded, standing and taking her bedroll from her pack.

"Just be careful to keep the fire burning brightly. I don't want to have an encounter with the Nibilus." She said as she rolled out her bed and laid down on it. Vesth nodded and turned his back to the fire, loosening the sword in his scabbard just in case he might have need of it.

He stood quietly watching the shifting shadows caused by the fire behind him. The night was clear and the forest swayed slightly at the touch of a breeze, and Vesth could tell that there was nothing near enough to the camp to cause trouble. His turn on watch was uneventful, only taking breaks to add wood to the fire. Near midnight he woke Rielle for her turn on watch and then laid down on his bedroll, his sword still close at hand.

"I feel that something is not quite right." He thought to himself, letting his eyes drift closed. *"I can't put my finger on it. It is like something is out of place, or incomplete."* Vesth squeezed his eyes shut, forcing the thoughts to disappear and clear his mind.

"Everything should be well as long as we follow Master Solidus's instructions." With this last thought Vesth slipped into light slumber.

13

Chapter Thirteen

Segine stepped out of the arena wearily, noticing Nysisset sitting at the plain wooden table helping herself to his dinner.

"That really wasn't much of a match." She told him, between mouthfuls of food. Segine grunted and sat heavily at the table, pulling his armor off and setting it aside. He looked at a broken rusty sword in his hand and tossed it aside in disgust.

"They keep giving me inferior blades. I told Tharis I would only fight using my weapon. These so called swords are no better than scrap." Nysisset shrugged, seemingly unconcerned.

"Well, you will be happy to hear you are being advanced to the next division of fighters. So you should get to use your own sword." Tharis entered the room with a huff.

"You are good, but don't get cocky. You will be fighting veterans from now on. Your next opponents have been here in the arena for a long time, and for good reason, so don't take them lightly if you want to survive." Segine just grunted, and started eating. Tharis watched quietly for a few moments before speaking again.

"Are you sure you want to keep pushing like this? You are barely getting enough rest as it is. Is getting your freedom by the new moon really that important to you?" Nysisset slowly turned and locked her blazing eyes on Tharis.

"We have three more days and the moon is nearly dark. If we are not free by then, this arena shall experience a blood bath that will make all other violence before it pale in comparison." Tharis did not flinch back from Nysisset's stare, but his frown said he took what she said seriously. After a moment's pause, he turned and began walking towards the exit.

"I want to see both of you in my quarters when you are finished eating. I wish to discuss your move to the next level of competition." Nysisset nodded and turned back to her food. Segine continued to eat, but his eyes carefully watched Nysisset. She ate gracefully, ignoring him for several minutes before placing an uneaten piece of bread back on the plate with a sigh.

"I am sorry." Segine's eyes widened and he paused for a moment.

"Why are you apologizing? That isn't like you at all." Segine said, also returning his food to its place on his plate. Nysisset looked back at the gate to the arena where the tiny sliver of light cast by the moon could be seen through the gaps.

"I know you don't like hearing me talk about slaughter and death." Segine felt his cheeks burn slightly.

"I do not approve of wanton death, but you do not need to apologize for speaking your thoughts." Nysisset turned back to Segine.

"But I spoke rashly. The Dark Moon Cycle approaches, and its power fills me with darkness. I am a Dark Angel, created by Lord Khornal, and even with my ties to him severed, darkness still courses through me." Segine remained silent, not sure what he was supposed to say. Nysisset looked back at the moon.

"On the night of the Dark Moon Cycle, I will not be myself. Stay out of my path on that night, give me room to fight and do not try to stop me." Segine frowned.

"But killing anyone will be unnecessary by then." Nysisset shook her head.

"Irrelevant. The darkness within me will take over and I will be filled with blood lust. The pendant I wear will give that power focus and erase everything else. I will know you as my companion and won't hurt you as long as you aren't in the way, so please..." Nysisset stood and turned away, closing her eyes.

"Don't let me hurt you." This said, she left. Segine sat quietly, unable to eat anything else. His thoughts turned slowly in his mind, mulling over every word. A servant came to retrieve him a short while later and he followed without complaint.

He was led out of the arena, across the training fields, and to the doorstep of a small hut that Tharis used as his office. The servant opened the door and waved him in before closing the door behind him. The hut was a single room filled with old weapons and bits of armor. At the other end of the room was a large table covered in papers, which Tharis quietly sat behind. Nysisset stood to one side of the table, frowning impatiently. Segine entered the room and stood next to Nysisset.

"I know who you are." Tharis stated simply. Segine raised one eyebrow and heard Nysisset huff. Tharis laced his fingers together and leaned his elbows on the table.

"I took your sword and made sure it was ready for battle and I recognized your family crest." Segine did his best to contain his surprise. Tharis spent a few moments thinking then looked up at Segine directly.

"You are the grandson of Marion Carsolia Memoria." Segine nearly choked.

"You know of my grandfather?" Tharis nodded.

"I had the opportunity to see him fight in a tournament. One of the last before his... accident." Segine growled quietly.

"It was no accident." Tharis growled right back.

"Don't you think I know that? Every knight in the realm at the time knew it was no accident, but there was no evidence to be had. But that is not what We are talking about right now." Tharis reached down beside the table and drew Segine's sword turning it to show the curled dragon at it's base.

"Are you worthy of this blade?" He asked. Segine stood tall and his features hardened.

"I earned that mark myself in tournament. The Knight King of Laytrow awarded it to me personally." Nysisset's eyes drifted to Segine momentarily, mildly surprised. Tharis nodded and dropped the sword back into it's scabbard. Then he looked at Nysisset.

"And you, young lady, I recognize you for what you are." Nysisset crossed her arms across her chest and stuck her nose in the air.

"I couldn't care less what you think I am." Tharis laced his fingers together again.

"You hail from the Mercury Mountains, am I wrong?" Segine looked at Nysisset, who continued to pout. Tharis sighed.

"I doubt anyone has yet noticed that your eyes have

gradually darkened the closer we come to the New Moon. And the tattoos on the sides of your neck are not ones of ink." Nysisset spared the knight a glance.

"And what would an old knight know of such things?" Tharis closed his eyes.

"I was once a trusted knight of the court, I know many things. But that is irrelevant now." Tharis sat back in his chair and looked at the two people across from him.

"Why do you want to get free?" Nysisset stuck her nose in the air again.

"Not that it has anything to do with you, but we have someone to find." Segine nodded. "And a mission to complete." Tharis's eyes narrowed.

"Who are you finding and what mission are you trying to complete?" Segine frowned, sealing his lips and shaking his head. Nysisset nodded, keeping her arms folded.

"I believe I mentioned that it has nothing to do with you." Tharis frowned as well.

"I am afraid I must inform you that you will not be free by the New Moon. I have been unable to convince any of the high bidders to sponsor you." Nysisset lowered her arms to her sides.

"Then are you prepared for the consequences?" She asked slowly. Segine nodded.

"You have had ample time to uphold your end of the deal, we will be free on the night of the Dark Moon Cycle with, or without, your help." Tharis nodded.

"This I am aware of, and I have made a decision." Nysisset half grinned, raising a hand before her.

"Oh? And what decision would that be, old knight? If you

really know what I am, then you know that stopping me is out of the question. My strength grows as the Dark Moon nears." Tharis nodded.

"Which is one reason why I have decided to aid in your escape." Nysisset lowered her hand, eyes widening slightly, and Segine was plainly shocked.

"Why would you do such a thing?" Tharis stood and faced away from them, looking out of a small window situated at eye level.

"I have decided I no longer wish to fight in this arena. I have heard plenty of rumors about what is going on in the rest of the continent. I think it would better suit me, and my fighters, to fight as mercenaries. At least then we might do a bit of good in the world." Segine frowned.

"Why the sudden change of heart?" Tharis laughed without enthusiasm.

"Just what makes you think my heart has changed?" Segine was taken aback. "I have always had the heart of a knight. This place has allowed me to grow strong, and train strong soldiers. In this way I can fight without the shame of losing my position as a knight in the royal court." Segine stared for several moments at the back of the old knight's head. He glanced at Nysisset, who simply shrugged, apparently bored with the conversation. Segine frowned again, unhappy with his current situation.

"Then what is your plan, Tharis Lionsmane?" Tharis turned.

"The plan is to continue fighting. I want you to move to the next level of competition." Segine grumbled.

"How is that going to do any good? You said yourself that no one will sponsor our freedom." Tharis nodded.

"True, but if you do not continue to fight then the patrons of the arena will become suspicious. The plan is this. I will convince the richest Patrons to agree to a true test of skill, where I pit all my fighters against any opponents of their choosing. It will be held the night of the New Moon. We will use this fight to spark chaos and confusion and use it as a cover for our escape." Segine thought over everything carefully.

"And what becomes of us once we are free?" Tharis waved one arm.

"Once we are outside the arena, you may go where you will. As I said, my men and I will become mercenaries. If you do not wish to join us, then that is your decision to make." Tharis picked up Segine's sword and held it out to him.

"Do you agree?" Nysisset placed one hand on Segine's shoulder and the knight shifted uncomfortably.

"Think about it carefully, Segine." She whispered. Segine thought about what she had told him about her bloodlust on the night of the Dark Moon. He nodded slowly.

"I will be sure to stay by your side. I am certain I can direct you so that you won't kill any innocents." Nysisset's grip on his shoulder tightened. He turned and looked her in the eye.

"You won't hurt me." He said, without doubt in his voice. Nysisset searched Segine's eyes for a moment and then nodded, letting go of his shoulder and turning to Tharis.

"We agree to your terms."

* * *

Segine opened his eyes, looking up at Nysisset in the late evening light. He immediately knew something was not right.

Nysisset was breathing heavily, her head leaned against the stone wall beside the bed. The tattoos on her neck were shifting ever so slightly, as if the snakes might take up a life of their own at any moment. Segine sat up and turned to face her.

"Is everything alright miss Nysisset?" Nysisset grunted in reply.

"I'm fine, knight." Segine frowned.

"You do not look fine." Nysisset opened one eye carefully and looked at him.

"I said I am fine. So that means I am fine." Segine continued to frown, and simply stared silently. Nysisset watched him for a few moments and then sighed in exasperation.

"If you must know, it is getting late and the Dark Moon is rising. I am simply struggling to control my power." Segine took the thin blanket that he had been sleeping under and tore a corner from it, wading it up and using it to carefully wipe away some of the sweat from Nysisset's forehead. Nysisset growled quietly at his touch, but Segine stubbornly continued.

"Go ahead and growl if it makes you feel better. But I won't let you struggle alone." Nysisset growled again, though more quietly, and opened her eye again to look at Segine. A knock came at their door and Tharis entered the room. Segine stood and faced the old knight.

"It is almost time." Segine nodded and looked back at Nysisset. She struggled to her feet, using the wall as support.

"Then let's get on with it." She said irritably. Tharis nodded.

"Very well. The fight will begin at full dark. My men will be waiting for you at the arena gates, so be sure to be geared up and ready to go. I have your armor prepared in my quarters. Make sure you have everything you want to take with you before you go to the gates, we won't be stopping once this starts." Segine nodded.

"I understand."

"Make sure you are ready yourself, old knight." Nysisset said darkly.

"With my pendant around my neck, I will lose control to my bloodlust when the Dark Moon reaches it's zenith. Be sure you have the main gates unlocked by then, unless you want everyone in the arena slaughtered." Tharis grunted.

"Don't you worry about me, I will stick to my part of the plan. Just focus on your own part." The old knight turned and stepped back out the door.

"Oh, and cover up those tattoos. If anyone notices them before the right time, the plan will fail." Nysisset growled at his back as he closed the door. Segine turned to look at Nysisset again.

"Are you sure you can make it until the moon has fully risen?" He asked. Nysisset laughed, a touch of madness marring her voice.

"Of course I will. It will be fun to string those fools along, not knowing what will happen to them when the moon has risen." She teetered on the edge of laughter again and looked up at Segine. He could see that her eyes were deepest violet, and they seemed to swallow all light that entered them. Nysisset slowly gained control of herself again and looked solemnly at Segine.

"Are you certain you can handle this? You are a knight, sworn to uphold honor at all times. Trying to direct me while I kill all in my path, can you really handle something like that? Do you think you can exert even the slightest influence over me once my reason has gone?" Segine's gaze hardened in a way that made the stone walls of their room seem soft.

"I will not forsake you. It is not a matter of If I can do it, I Will direct you. It would be far more damaging to my honor if I abandoned my companions. You are no exception, regardless of what state of mind you may be in." Nysisset grumbled, but the slightest of smiles touched her lips.

"You may change your mind once I change. My teeth will become long and sharp, My skin will become pale, and My tattoos will become living weapons. Not to mention the darkness that will flow from my body, made stronger by my amulet." Nysisset touched the shining black stone chained around her neck. Nysisset breathed in sharply as the stone reacted to her touch and power raced down her arm. Segine took hold of her hand and firmly pulled it away from the stone.

"I think you should refrain from touching it until it is time to act." Nysisset studied Segine's features for a moment and then quickly pulled her arm away from him.

"You don't have to tell me. I am all too aware of how powerful it is." Segine said nothing, but lifted the thin blanket in his hands and tore a long thin strip from it and held it out to Nysisset.

"Here, use this to cover your tattoos." Nysisset looked at the strip of torn cloth disdainfully.

"Now you are beginning to sound like Master Solidus." She took it and carefully tied it around her neck, covering the writhing snakes. Segine shrugged and lifted his sword from beside the bed and walked towards the door.

"I will do as Tharis suggested and gather my armor from his quarters."

"Do you think it will help you any? There are some things that armor simply cannot protect you from." Segine nodded, opening the door.

"I will wear it all the same. As I said, regardless of what may happen to me, I will not abandon you." He closed the door behind him and Nysisset stood in the center of the room quietly. She shook her head to clear the red from her vision and thoughts, and felt a faint sense of calm. She huffed and the slight smile returned.

"Foolish knight."

* * *

"Can you fight as well as they tell me you can Soul Reaper?" The larger of the two men beside Segine asked. Segine grunted.

"You have trained with me for weeks, and I have survived the arena this long, what makes you doubt my skills now?" The man looked down at Segine through the slit in his helmet.

"I want to make sure the man who has my back won't fall and leave me exposed." Segine grunted again.

"How many formations has Tharis taught you?" The large man looked back at the arena gate, through which they could hear the roar of the crowd.

"Hundreds. The Ironfelt, Coharen, and Memoria disciplines. Including the three man formation from the Memoria strategies that we will be using to survive this battle. Why do you ask?" Segine half smiled as the announcer introduced the next fight and the arena gates swung open. Segine took a step and led the way into the pit.

"My sur-name is Memoria." Segine heard the big man's breath catch, and half smiled before catching himself.

"I shouldn't take pleasure in such things. I think I may have

spent too much time listening to Nysisset." He thought to himself, before the announcer's ever annoying voice interrupted all other thoughts.

"And Finally, the event everyone has been waiting to witness, and the final fight of the evening." The crowd roared and many leapt to their feet.

"Depraved souls. Have they nothing better to do?" Segine muttered.

"Not likely." The large man said simply.

"Let me introduce tonight's fighters." The announcer continued. "First, a man who never speaks, who never yells, who never so much as whispers. A man who lives in the silence and destroys any who breaks that silence. Nemian the Silencer!" Segine glanced over his shoulder and the short stocky man beside him.

"Better a man of silence, than a man too fond of his own voice." Segine muttered, and the man nodded in agreement.

"Next, A giant of a man, capable of smashing boulders with his bare hands. A man whose power is simple, unrefined, and utterly unstoppable. Karnash the Crusher!" Segine looked up at the large man on his other side.

"I am not sure whether or not that should be taken as an insult." The large man nodded, and Segine could tell he was grinning.

"We shall show them tonight who is 'Simple' and 'Unrefined'." Segine nodded and turned, his features hardening as the crowd roared again.

"And last, but by far not the least, The man who prays for the souls of those who will die, before mercilessly cutting them down. The man who has risen through the levels of this arena faster than any other before him save his master, Tharis Lionsmane. The man who we cannot decide if he is a demon or a saint. Soul Reaper Segine!" Segine tightened his grip on his sword at his hip as the entire crowd rose to their feet and the cheers became deafening.

"Tonight, as with the moon, they shall see my darker side. And just once, will I strive to fulfill the title Soul Reaper." Once the crowd had begun to settle down, the announcer spoke again.

"These three men, The elites trained by Tharis Lionsmane himself, will face a challenge tonight the likes of which have never before been seen in this arena. They will fight ten men, with odds greater than three against one, who have been hand picked by the V.I.P's to give us the greatest amount of entertainment that can possibly be gleaned from a single fight." The gates all around the arena began to open and movement could be seen behind them.

"Take up formation." Segine said, drawing his sword and holding it firmly in both hands. The large man adjusted the massive tower shield on one arm and then drew a longsword with his other, stepping into a position behind and to one side of Segine and using his size to take up as much space as possible. The shorter man took a small round shield from his back and strapped it to his arm, then drew a long knife. He turned and faced outward from the other two, setting himself behind his small shield and forming a triangle with the other men.

The gates swung fully open and for a single moment, there was calm and a stillness that set the nerves on edge. Then the stillness was shattered as men rushed in from all sides, war cries tearing from their throats. Segine watched each of the men rushing him carefully as they drew closer. Segine waited until they were only a few paces away before shouting an order.

"Expand and Contract!" As one, the three men stepped forward out of their formation and struck. The large man met four men head on and knocked them down, using his shield as a battering ram.

Segine jumped and, with his own battle cry, brought his sword down hard. The force of the blow crushed the helmet of one of the men, and knocked him into another, sending both to the ground. The third man struck at Segine, aiming to take off his head. Segine twisted, easily intercepting the man's attack, and twisted his sword so the man could see the crouching dragon at the base of the blade. The man choked and took a half step back. Segine sensed the movement and quickly felled the man with a powerful blow from one of his fists.

The shorter man jumped forward, bashed one man across the face with his shield, intercepted a sword with the shield in the same motion, and easily slashed the throat of a third attacker. All three men jumped back and re-assumed their formation.

"What a devastating first blow!" The announcer yelled excitedly. "Magnificent team work. Truly Tharis Lionsmane has trained a team that could easily handle military trained soldiers. I wonder how many of their attackers will have made it through this initial strike." The men around them slowly began to stand and recover. Four men remained on the ground, unmoving. Two were bleeding, and one of them was most definitely dead. The remaining men were acting cautiously, and slowly circling around Segine and the other two.

"Tortoise defense until attacked." Segine ordered, switching his stance so that his sword covered most of his body. The large man lifted his shield, completely hiding behind it. Only his eyes glared out over the top of the shield, daring his enemies to attack. The shorter man crouched low, hiding behind his small shield and raising his knife over his head. They closed in to each other, shrinking their formation until they were nearly standing back to back. Two fighters leapt at the large man, and another followed close behind.

"Snake strike!" Segine called. The large man raised his shield over his head and ran one of the fighters through with his longsword. Segine slipped his sword under the large man's arm and let the second fighter run onto his blade. The shorter man twisted under the shield and buried his knife into the side of the third fighter before he had a chance to retreat. Segine turned and deflected an attack from behind and then they all slipped back into formation.

"Oh, another deadly clash." The announcer called out, clearly enjoying himself. "It seems that the odds are more equal now than when we started."

"He seems to be right." The large man stated looking at the three remaining fighters that continued to circle.

"Would you be against some single combat?" Segine asked. The shorter man merely shook his head.

"I am willing to fight on my own. They are pretty weak after all." The large man said. Segine nodded.

"Break formation." The three men stepped forward, each coming face to face with one of the remaining fighters.

"No more teamwork?" The announcer asked, feigning shock. "These fighters must be getting serious." The remaining fighters jumped in all at once and attacked, and each of them were struck down mid-stride.

"Truly this is a glorious occasion." The announcer called out to the cheering crowd. "Never has such a fight been seen in this arena, and it has set a new precedent." Segine watched as the rotund man in the rich booths stood and made his way to the rail that overlooked the pit, the area behind his chair shrouded in palpable darkness.

"Toward the back wall." Segine muttered quietly to the other two. Each slowly backed up without any other gestures and waited as the rotund man cleared his throat.

"Who says that we cannot be further entertained?" The crowd chattered to one another. Segine carefully looked at the sky and then back at the man.

"I suggest the fight continue since it does not seem it was too difficult for our fine fighters to lay low their enemies. I have twenty more men waiting to fight, if the Elite of Tharis Lionsmane think they can handle it." Segine looked at the other two.

"When they come, form a two man formation against the back wall and stay there until my companion and I have left. You will die otherwise." The larger man grumbled, but both nodded. Segine turned and looked back up at the man.

"We can handle any fight." Segine called up. "I ask only one thing in return." The rotund man grinned and motioned, the arena gates opened and more men entered the pit. Segine notice the large main gate cracked open and Tharis waved at him, signaling that everything was ready. The two men behind Segine pressed their backs against the wall and raised their shields.

"What do you ask for in return for fighting?" The rotund man asked. Segine took a deep breath and then hardened his features, pointing the tip of his large sword at the man.

"I ask only for... Your Soul." Many of the fighters in the pit stopped cold, the crowd laughed nervously, and the rotund man sputtered slightly.

"What do you mean my soul? It is stuck inside my body, I can't simply give it away. I am afraid I am just too attached to it." He said, trying to make light of the demand. Segine took one look at the sky and then back at the man.

"Not for long. Your soul is no longer yours." The rotund man's face became angry, but before he could say anything, something sharp and black pierced through his chest. Then he was thrown from the booth to land face first on the pit floor. The entire arena was silent. On the railing of the booth stood a creature dressed all in black, jet black hair waving in the wind, with tendrils of darkness trailing from their back and chest.

"Behold," Segine called out in an icy cold voice, placing the final piece. "The True Soul Reaper!" Panic ensued.

The people in the crowd screamed and scrambled over one another, trying to escape the viewing booths. The fighters ran, some towards Segine and the other two men, some towards the rotund man, and the rest towards the exits.

Nysisset leapt from the rail and landed on the shoulders of two fighters running towards the main exit. With an elegant twist, she slashed their throats with black blades she held in each hand, and dropped to the ground. Segine watched Tharis open the main gate and then set himself against the wall with a broadsword and a large knight's shield.

Nysisset continued to race amongst the fighters, killing any unfortunate enough to get within arm's reach.

"Soldiers are pouring into the arena to try and deal with the chaos." Tharis yelled to Segine. "If you don't move fast we will get overrun." Segine wasted no time in racing to Nysisset and placing himself between her and a fighter she was closing in on.

"Wait Nysisset." Segine yelled, his voice hard as stone. Nysisset skidded to a stop and pondered him carefully. Two fangs peaked out from her pale lips, sharp as needles, and giving Segine an uneasy twinge in his stomach.

"You want to fight? You want blood?" He asked. Nysisset said nothing, but her eyes went completely black and she cocked her head to one side, obviously understanding what Segine said.

"I know where you can find more worthy opponents than the scum here." Nysisset grinned, showing that the rest of her teeth were now just as sharp as her fangs, and the dark tendrils around her became excited.

"Show me." Nysisset rasped, her voice twisting as it left her throat. Segine felt a pang in his chest and he pointed to the main gate.

"Through there. Many strong soldiers want to keep you here. They want to control you, and keep you away from the forest. Will such a powerful creature as you accept this?" Nysisset growled, a dark and ominous sound.

"They will pay." Nysisset rasped angrily. She turned and raced towards the gate, running as if she were weightless. Segine followed as closely behind as he could, sword at the ready. He slowed as he passed Tharis.

"Follow us, but stay back far enough to be out of sight. And try to escape in the opposite direction that Nysisset chooses to take." Tharis nodded knocking a fighter off his feet with his shield.

"Take care, Segine Memoria, I hope we meet again under better circumstances." Segine placed his fist over his heart in salute, then raced off after Nysisset.

14

Chapter Fourteen

Rielle's hand rested nervously on her sword as Vesth inspected the skeletal remains. He touched his fingers to the ground and then brought them to his nose. Rielle stood still, carefully watching their surroundings, and feeling something strange as a slight breeze flitted across her skin.

"So?" She asked. Vesth stood and looked at the two enormous trees standing before them.

"I am uncertain what killed him. One of his legs is broken, but it isn't bad enough to be what finished him. It is difficult to tell with nothing but bones, But I am certain that he was trying to get away from there." He pointed at the two trees. Rielle nodded.

"The entrance to the Temple of Wind is there. The trees once guarded the entrance, now they have overgrown it." Vesth stared into the narrow space between the trees before shivering and turning to Rielle.

"Are you certain we must enter there miss Rielle?" Rielle nodded.

"There is no other way. But I think we should be cautious. I do not like the feeling this place gives me." Vesth nodded.

"I also feel something out of place here. I will lead the way." Rielle nodded and Vesth squeezed between the two trees. They followed a narrow corridor of stone. Most of the ceiling had collapsed or eroded away due to the plant growth, so they found that torches and lanterns were unnecessary.

Vesth carefully picked his way through the dead leaves and tree roots that littered the floor, his hand carefully placed on his sword. When they came to the other end of the corridor they found a stone doorway, faded symbols and pictographs etched into its surface. Vesth turned and slid carefully into the doorway and craned his neck to see inside. He immediately froze and his hand tightened on his sword. Rielle took notice and the hand resting on her own sword tightened instantly.

"What's wrong Vesth?" Vesth was silent for several moments before turning his head to look at Rielle, worry in his eyes.

"We should not have come here." Fear gripped at Rielle's stomach. Slowly, she walked to the doorway and peered down into the room below. It was littered with corpses. Rielle brought a hand to her mouth to prevent a scream from escaping her lips. There were bones scattered around the room, a few with papery skin still clinging to them, but many of the bodies were fresh. Some halfway through decomposing, others could only have been dead for a day or two at the most.

In the center of the room was a makeshift altar of stacked stones with a large flat stone placed on top of the pile. Bolted into this stone were shackles at both ends and swirling grooves were carved into it's surface.

"What happened here?" Rielle spoke hoarsely, fear still

lodged in her throat. Vesth peered over the room with his eyes and then glanced over his shoulder and scanned the way they had come.

"Rituals were performed here. And experiments on human bodies." He stated looking back at the room. Rielle choked for a moment before regaining her senses.

"What do you mean, rituals and experiments?" Vesth stared blankly at the altar.

"Rituals designed to force the magical potential held within a human to mix with the physical energy of the body. It creates incredible physical ability, but the body cannot handle the strain and inevitably tears itself apart." Rielle looked over the bodies with a horrified expression.

"Is that what happened to all of them?" Vesth remained still.

"Most of them. The man who made it outside broke his leg on the way out, his body was unable to handle the strength and the bone most likely snapped under the pressure. But some of these people were simply sacrificed." Rielle felt her stomach knot.

"Who would do such a thing?" Vesth looked back over his shoulder.

"Whoever they are will likely be back. Many of the bodies are fresh, so they probably return every night. We should leave immediately." Rielle shook herself.

"No, we can't leave yet. We still have to visit the seal chamber. We cannot leave this undone." Rielle could see Vesth struggle inwardly, his eyes passing from the room, to the exit, to the sky above them, and back to the room. Eventually he loosed his sword in it's scabbard.

"We should hurry." Rielle nodded sharply and entered the

room. They skirted around the edge of the room, Rielle muttering apologies and prayers to the bodies they stepped over, Vesth simply glancing unhappily at them and making the sign to ward away evil.

At the other end of the room, Rielle fumbled around looking for a lever, making a small victory noise as she found and pulled it. There was a low grinding noise, and the stone floor beside them sank. Vesth jumped to one side before realizing the stones were forming a narrow, spiral stairway. They followed them down and found themselves walking out into a large room that was remarkably similar to the one they had seen in the Temple of Balance.

Rielle made her way to the altar in the center of the room and knelt beside it, clasping her hands and bowing her head in a silent prayer. Vesth placed himself directly behind her and turned back to face the stairway, readying his sword in case it was needed. The wait was a long one, and each passing minute put Vesth more and more on edge. More than an hour later he heard Rielle stir.

"Are you finished here?" Rielle stood and shook her head slowly.

"The only word I hear when I petition the Deity of Wind is 'Defiled', repeated over and over again. I cannot get through to her." Vesth spared a glance back to Rielle.

"Then we should leave and get a safe distance from the temple to spend the night. We can return tomorrow." Rielle nodded and then froze as she looked up. Vesth swung around and saw two men standing standing at the base of the stairs, one in an opulent velvet robe.

"Magnificent." The man in the robe said, as he looked around the room. "I had no idea such a room dwelt below the temple. Truly this is providence." The second man nodded.

"Truly prophet. But what of our guests?" The robed man looked at Vesth and Rielle.

"Two children should not be in such a sacred place. Erase them, Erados." The man named Erados nodded and drew a longsword from his side. Vesth drew his sword in response and Rielle did the same, though a pace behind Vesth. Both men eyed one another for a few moments and then the man Erados charged them.

Vesth raced out to meet him and their swords rang as they clashed. Vesth slid past the man and spun around just in time to intercept another blow. Vesth grunted under the weight of Erados' sword.

"Your blows are heavy." Vesth managed. The man Erados nodded.

"I have been granted divine strength by the prophet. The fact that you could even stand against such strength is impressive." Vesth grunted and pushed the man back.

"So you have had your first gate opened then." Erados struck again and Vesth chose to deflect the attack rather than meet it head on, Then reversed his blade and struck Erados a blow to the chin with the butt of his sword. Erados stumbled back a pace and rubbed his chin.

"You are quite skilled." Vesth raised his sword again and said nothing.

"What is wrong Erados? Is this child too much for you?" The robed man asked. Erados shook his head.

"No, Prophet, I was merely caught off guard. This one is quite skilled, and he is strong enough to meet my divine strength head on." The robed man looked mildly surprised.

"Truly now? Perhaps the heavens smile down on us more than I had thought. Deal with the other one, we shall use this one in the ritual tonight." Erados nodded and half turned towards Rielle. Vesth's eyes flashed angrily and his sword moved in a blur of motion. Erados turned, caught Vesth's sword with the edge of his own, and flicked it away. Vesth did not lose his sword, but the force of the deflection was so great that it threw him off balance and he felt a searing pain as Erados's sword landed a grazing blow to his off hand shoulder.

Vesth landed on his back with a pained grunt and he heard Rielle scream his name. Erados spared him a glance and then turned back to Rielle. Rielle raised her sword, ready to defend herself. Erados swayed back and forth a few times and then charged her at full speed. Rielle gasped and then felt as if time slowed around her and an incredible weight settled on her shoulders.

"*It is they who defiled my temple.*" Rielle heard the whispers in her mind.

"Soaring Zephyr Sidhe?" Rielle asked hopefully, but the voice ignored her.

"*I will help you destroy them, student of the Silver Mage, But only if you cleanse my temple.*" Rielle nodded, watching as Erados slowly drew closer, his sword raising to strike.

"I will cleanse your temple, Great Sidhe, if only you will reveal to me how." Rielle felt power enter her limbs and time seemed to return to normal again.

"With Fire." Rielle heard. She nodded and gripped her sword. Erados reached her in the blink of an eye and his strike was almost impossible to see. Without thinking, Rielle twisted nimbly out of the way and raised her sword defensively.

"You are fast." Erados stated, turning and striking again. Rielle felt her body loosen, and when she moved, it was even faster than before. She deflected his attack away from her and then twisted and slashed at his unprotected back. Her sword bit deeply into his thick clothing, but not deeply enough to touch flesh. Erados twisted around and swatted her blade away from him, nearly causing her to loose the sword. Erados shrugged his shoulders, testing his clothing.

"You are indeed fast. If you also had strength I would no doubt loose to you. But your speed will do you little good without the strength to administer the final blow." Erados raised his sword, as if to strike, but paused as a croak was heard behind him.

"Wait." Vesth struggled to his feet with a pained expression. "Your battle is with me." Vesth reversed his grip on the sword in his good hand and raised it in front of him, cradling his injured arm against his body. Erados frowned at Vesth then looked to the robed man.

"Prophet?" The robed man sighed.

"If he will not lie quietly, then you may do what you must Erados." Erados bowed and then started towards Vesth.

"This time I will end you with one strike." Vesth bowed his head and closed his eyes.

"Be sure you do, because if your first strike does not kill me, you will not have the chance for a second." Erados raced at Vesth, sword raised to kill. As the blade dropped, Rielle felt the slightest of ripples, that seemed to come from within Vesth. Vesth vanished and Erados's blade met nothing but air.

He turned and attacked again. Vesth appeared before Erados and knocked his sword from his hands and then twisted and planted his blade deeply into the man's side. Erados coughed and stumbled backwards, taking a few steps before falling to his knees.

"It seems, you also have divine strength." He rasped. Vesth shook his head.

"There is nothing divine about it. If it is, then it is a divine curse." The robed man looked stunned.

"Someone outside the sect who has opened the gates? Un-acceptable!" Rage filled his features and he raised his hand into the air. "Unacceptable!!" He screamed, calling fire to his hand.

Rielle barely had time to raise her own hand and build a barrier around Vesth as the man threw the fireball at him. The fire struck the barrier and Rielle quickly twisted her hand and, with a shout, extinguished the flames. The robed man spun to look at her in utter shock.

"*Kill Him!*" Rielle acted on the command instinctively, rushing the man. The air felt heavy against her as she moved, twisting her sword to pierce the man's chest, cracking the wall behind him as he struck it and her blade cut through him and into the wall.

"For tainting the Temple of Wind, your life is forfeit." She told the dying man in a low voice. She removed the sword and let him fall, landing one final strike to end him as he hit the ground. She wiped her sword off on her blood spattered clothing and then placed it in it's scabbard, turning to walk up the stairs.

"Wait, where are you going?" Vesth called, a sharp breath of pain cutting his sentence a little short. "There are likely still cult members up there." Rielle didn't stop.

"I will cleanse the temple." She said, raising her arms. Several balls of fire appeared around her and spun through the air, as if waiting to be directed. Vesth tried to go after her, but swayed as he felt exhaustion and pain fill his senses. He stumbled, dropping his sword and landing face down on the stone floor.

* * *

Vesth struggled through the haze of his dreams and tried to open his eyes. At first he saw nothing, then blurred shapes, and eventually his eyes focused and he found himself lying beside a small fire. Vesth sat up, wincing as pain shot through his shoulder.

"Easy there." A familiar voice told him. "I just patched you up, don't go tearing the wound open again." Vesth cradled his left arm and turned his head to see Solidus sitting beside the fire, prodding at it with a short stick.

"Master Solidus? What are you doing here?" Solidus continued to prod.

"While I was going about my other business I felt a shift in the balance here. When I arrived you were unconscious in the seal chamber, and Rielle was reducing everything in the antechamber to ash." Vesth felt a small shock travel through him.

"Where is miss Rielle?" He asked, looking around the fire, hoping to find her. Worry filled his mind when he did not.

"She is sleeping." Solidus said, adding a few more sticks to the small fire. "She used a good deal of energy in the temple, and using the Cloak of a Deity puts great strain on one's body."

"Is she well?" Vesth asked immediately. Solidus smiled.

"She is well, she just needs rest. When she wakes you will need to continue on your way to the Temple of Water." Vesth stood and positioned himself on a root of a nearby tree.

"Will you not be traveling with us?" Solidus shook his head.

"No. I have other things to attend to. And I must start with the temple here. The defilement of the temple weakened its strength, and it has not been tended to in quite some time. And with Soaring Zephyr Sidhe bringing her presence into the temple to speak with Rielle, the balance in this place is disturbed. I will have to bring things back into balance before I can leave." Vesth listened silently, watching the fire twist and flow across the wood it consumed.

Things were calm and quiet in the forest, and Vesth found his mind wandering placidly without any real direction. He didn't like it. He quickly shook his head and tried to find something to focus on.

"You mentioned something before about the Cloak of a Deity. What is it exactly?" Solidus continued to poke at the fire with his stick, watching Vesth out of the corner of his eye.

"The Cloak of a Deity is a type of magic that covers or cloaks the user's body with the element of that Deity and gives them unique strengths. The Cloak of Sidhe, or the Cloak of Wind if you prefer, allows the user to move very quickly. The air parts around them and does not slow them down as they move. Soaring Zephyr Sidhe gave Rielle her Cloak to help her fight the one who attacked you. In return, Rielle burned everything within the temple that was not meant to be there, attempting to cleanse it." Vesth thought back to the fight in the temple, he had been in a fog because of his injury and his use of the second gate, but it seemed like he remembered Rielle closing the distance to the prophet in an almost impossibly short amount of time.

"So Rielle was Cloaked in wind and that is what allowed her to move faster?" Solidus nodded.

"Yes, it is a very rare skill to be able to use." Then Vesth felt an incredibly sharp pain in his abdomen, lancing through his entire body. He doubled over, arms wrapped around his stomach, doing everything he could to prevent a gasp of pain from escaping his lips.

Then a hand reached out and lifted his head. Solidus knelt on the ground in front of Vesth and gently pulled his hands away from his stomach. Solidus placed one hand on Vesth's forehead, and one on his stomach, then carefully pressed. Immediately Vesth felt ice flow through his body, chilling him to the bone. The pain slowly subsided, and Solidus stood, brushing the dirt and leaves from his knees. Vesth shivered and tried to scoot closer to the small fire. Solidus returned to his seat on an old stump and added some wood to the fire.

"You should be more careful about opening your gates." Solidus spoke quietly. "Forcing them open like that will do you more harm than good. At the least you should have used your key." Vesth nodded.

"I know, But I didn't have any other options. I was injured and my opponent's strength was too great for me to meet head on."

"And you wished to protect Rielle no matter the cost." Solidus stated. Vesth nodded.

"It is the reason I came on this journey. I feel obligated to protect her, even if she is able to do so on her own." Solidus gave Vesth a sly glance.

"I wonder why that could be." Vesth knew that Solidus was making fun of him, but he couldn't quite figure out how. He rubbed his hands together and held them out to the fire. Solidus sighed.

"If you still insist on using the gates to protect Rielle, then you better start training your body to resist the power that flows from them." Vesth looked at Solidus and saw a serious look on his face that made Vesth feel that Solidus knew something important that remained unspoken.

"Train?" He asked. Solidus nodded. "The power behind the Nine Gates is the power of life itself. It flows through you and affects everything you do. It creates energy that flows through your body, and power behind the force of magic. But if too much is released too quickly, the body cannot handle the power and it is torn apart. The body must be trained to withstand this power so that greater strength can be used." Vesth's hands tightened into fists and he turned to Solidus.

"How?"

15

Chapter fifteen

Nysisset woke, cheeks burning as if she had sat too long in the sun. She opened her eyes and the light of a camp fire told her she also had a splitting headache. She closed her eyes again and thought back to the night of the Dark Moon Cycle.

She remembered everything through a red haze after she lost control at the moon's zenith. She felt herself start to smile at the thought of the blood on her hands, then frowned, as she thought of Segine seeing that smile. She remembered a shapeless form, that she felt had been Segine, directing her actions as she rampaged. Telling her where her enemies were surely hiding from her, or where they planned to stop her from doing as she pleased. She followed each direction with only thoughts of slaughter and death to fill the void of her mind.

"Clever, knight." She muttered to herself, half disdainfully, half impressed. She heard a motion in front of her, across the fire, and recognized Segine's footsteps.

"Are you well?" She heard him ask. His voice was gruff, but kind.

"I am well enough, knight." She answered without opening her eyes. She realized her voice was a bit raspy. Apparently Segine noticed as well.

"Are you thirsty?" Nysisset sighed, already frustrated with the simple knight.

"Of course I am. But I will not open my eyes or lift my head until my skull does not feel like it has been cleaved in two." She heard Segine grumble like he was nodding his head. She heard him shuffling around and then return to her side.

"Open your mouth." He told her, and she felt several drops of cool water fall on her lips. She parted her lips and felt a thin stream of water fill her dry mouth and throat. She swallowed several times and then the stream stopped and she heard Segine stand and move again.

Nysisset chanced opening one of her eyes to a narrow slit, careful to look away from the fire, and found she was laying on a narrow bedroll in a dark place she could not identify.

"Where are we?" Her voice sounded better than before, but her throat was sore from being dry for so long.

"A few miles from the base of the Mercury Mountains, in a large hallow tree." Nysisset's eye slid around behind her lid and she looked around as best she could. Segine returned to her side and held a small cup to her lips.

"Drink." He told her. Nysisset opened her mouth and tasted a bitter liquid flow into her mouth. She grimaced and then another cup was pressed to her lips.

"And again." He said, but Nysisset pressed her lips together stubbornly.

"Drink." Segine repeated firmly. Nysisset growled but drank the bitter liquid. A third time a cup was placed against her lips.

"Once more." Nysisset grumbled, knowing she would not win an argument with a stone wall, and thinking of several ways to get back at the knight. She parted her lips and a sweet liquid washed away the bitterness in her mouth.

"Your headache should pass quickly." Segine said, standing and walking away again.

"So you practice herbal medicine now, knight?" Nysisset tried to look through the narrow space of her eyelids, trying to see where Segine had gone.

"All knights are given training in basic healing herbs. The plains have very little in the way of herbs, but if one is ever stranded in foreign lands the knowledge can be useful." Nysisset grumbled, sorry she had asked.

"So what do you plan to do now knight?" She asked, hoping the answer would not be too long.

"The plan was to find Captain Vesth and Miss Rielle after we escaped was it not?" Nysisset grumbled.

"And how do you plan to do that knight? They could be anywhere in Galbrea. Do you want to search under every tree and rock to find them?" She heard him huff unhappily.

"Of course not, but we have to find them somehow. How would you suggest we proceed?" Nysisset momentarily thought of returning to the Mercury mountains, but dismissed the idea almost immediately.

"Well, we know they were headed for the Mercury Mountains when we left Alenon. I suspect they were going to visit one of the temples located on the southern face of the mountains."

"Then perhaps we should begin our search there." Segine suggested. Nysisset grumbled.

"It has been weeks since we fell off the ship. They will have moved on already. Besides, the only reason you made it through the mountains on your first visit was because Master Solidus was with you. If you tried to enter the mountains again the beasts there would tear you apart, so don't be daft, knight." Nysisset heard Segine grumble, obviously hurt.

"Then what should we do?" Nysisset growled in aggravation.

"You have a brain, Use it! I can't do everything for you. We know they were likely going to visit a temple, and so it is logical to believe they would be traveling to other temples as well. But I have lived my life in the protection of the Mercury Mountains. I do not know where the elemental temples are located, So do not ask me how to find them." There was silence for a long while and then Nysisset heard movement.

"I am going out to gather more firewood and to think on a solution to our problem. If you feel like eating there are a few travel rations that Tharis provided us in a pack against the tree trunk." Nysisset listened to Segine leave their shelter until his footsteps faded away.

"Finally, some quiet." Nysisset carefully rolled over and rested her head on her arm. She rested comfortably for a while and grudgingly admitted that Segine's bitter tasting medicine seemed to be working. She lay there, resting quietly, for several hours. It wasn't until she felt the air cool as the sun began to set that she heard Segine return.

He entered their shelter, dropping an armload of firewood near the door. She waited quietly as he carefully coaxed some buried coals back to life and added wood to start the fire ablaze. Nysisset felt herself start to smile as she basked in the fire's warmth, but made sure to carefully conceal it from Segine. She heard him shuffle around a little more before finally settling down beside the fire.

"Will you be ready to travel by tomorrow?" He asked after a few moments. Nysisset sighed, having hoped he would think she was asleep.

"I am more than ready." Segine was silent for a few more moments.

"Tomorrow we should head for Terramine." Nysisset opened one eye in surprise. "The Capital of Hortaal? Why?" Segine prodded the small fire with a stick.

"The High King there is miss Rielle's cousin. He may be willing to help us locate the temples. And there is always the chance that Rielle and Vesth may pass through there on their way to these temples. If that is so we will be able to discover where they were headed and how far we are behind them."

"That is what you came up with on your walk?" Nysisset asked, though she admitted to her self that the plan was a sound one.

"It is a logical course of action and will narrow our search significantly." Nysisset shrugged as if she didn't care and closed her eyes again.

"Do as you wish, it is better than no plan at all." Segine grunted, but did not reply.

* * *

Vesth kept a careful eye on the forest around them as he followed a few paces behind Rielle. They walked slowly, being careful to avoid anything they thought could hinder them or lead an enemy to track them more easily.

"Is going into Terramine a wise decision?" Vesth asked as

he carefully stepped around some dead leaves so as not to crush them.

"We won't make good time on foot. We need to procure some horses and some more supplies before we try heading to the Temple of Water." Rielle answered, trying to avoid crushing the sparse vegetation beneath the trees. Vesth nodded.

"I understand that, but there are a great many people in Terramine. Some of them are sure to have ties to those who are trying to find us. Would it not be wise to stop in a smaller town or city?" Rielle was silent for a short time as they walked, thinking until they finally reached a break in the trees and they found themselves on the edge of the vast plain around Terramine.

"Terramine is the only place we are guaranteed to find what we need. Besides I feel. . . drawn there somehow. As if something there is calling me to find it." Rielle paused as she stared at the stone city. Vesth did not like it. The way Rielle had said something was calling to her made him uncomfortable and he felt it was not wise to seek it out. But he realized it was not an argument he was going to win so he nodded obediently.

"Very well then, but let us hurry. Something in the air here makes me feel tense, as if there is something here that does not belong. Rielle turned and looked at Vesth, immediately seeing the discomfort behind his eyes. She sniffed at the air, and it seemed to buzz. It smelled almost metallic and caused bile to rise in her throat.

"I think you are right. Something does seem out of place." Vesth nodded and took the lead, out across the field.

"Then let us not waste any more time." Rielle followed closely behind her eyes scanning the area. She felt as if something was watching her as she walked. They hurried across the open land and entered the small gate on the west side of the city.

"I think it prudent to split up." Vesth said looking around the busy streets. "We will be able to gather what we need more quickly. I will find the horses we need if you will gather the other supplies we need for travel. While you do, you can also look for whatever was calling to you." Rielle nodded quietly, a distant expression on her face. Vesth stepped directly in front of her and made her make eye contact with him before he spoke again.

"Whether you find it or not, we should meet back here in an hour and be gone before nightfall." Rielle nodded slowly.

"I understand. If you think that is the best course of action I will defer to your wisdom." Vesth slowly exhaled and fixed Rielle with an unwavering stare.

"Are you well, miss Rielle? You have been acting a little strangely since the Temple of Wind." Rielle blinked once.

"What do you mean? I feel fine." Vesth sighed and stepped away.

"If you say so, then I will not force the matter. I am just a little worried about you, that's all." Rielle's distant look faded away for a moment, and her cheeks blushed a soft rose color.

"Thank you, Vesth. I promise that I am well. We should hurry." Vesth half bowed to Rielle and then turned and headed down one street.

"One hour." He repeated as he left. Rielle nodded her acknowledgment and then chose a different street to begin her search. Vesth moved quickly, heading for the stables in hopes of finding some horses for purchase. But as he drew near the stableyard a voice called out and stopped him.

"Ho there young man. Do you seek a fine steed to travel with?" Vesth slowed and turned toward the sound of the voice. Down a wide street that appeared to circle around the stableyard sat a man with a cart and four horses tied to posts beside it.

"I can cut you a fair price if you purchase two." Vesth looked around, no one seemed to be around, and something about the man made him very nervous.

"I just so happen to be looking for fair mounts good sir." Vesth called out, though he chose not to get any closer to the man and his cart. The man chuckled and nodded excitedly.

"Oh excellent, excellent. I have two fine horses right here if you are interested." Vesth eyed the mounts, something about them seemed strange.

"We will need to be traveling a long distance, will these mounts be able to handle a fast pace for several days?" Again, the man nodded. He slipped away from his cart and took hold of the reigns of two of his horses and slowly walked to the end of the street. Vesth did not touch his sword, but he half turned in case he needed to draw it.

"Look over these two horses here young man, I think you will find that they suit your needs just fine." The man stayed a respectful distance away and held the reigns out to Vesth. Vesth cautiously took the reigns and then placed a hand on one of the horses noses. He immediately knew what had caused him to think they were strange.

"These horses, I have seen them before." The man winked, and Vesth noticed an intelligent twinkle behind his eyes.

"You left the poor things to wander around in the plains

after you chose to go through Lord Tiamat's lair." Vesth felt some of his tension leave his body.

"So it is you, Master Delgorin." The man chuckled and placed a finger against his lips.

"Don't tell anyone now, I am in hiding after all." Vesth nodded hurriedly.

"Of course Master Delgorin. I will not speak of it." Delgorin nodded and then his face grew serious.

"And what of young Rielle?" Vesth looked back the way he had come.

"We split up to gather supplies more quickly. She also said something here was calling to her and she needed to find it." Vesth's fist tightened slightly around the reigns. Delgorin noticed and looked to the sky.

"There is a presence here, one I have not felt in quite some time." Vesth looked at the old man out of the corner of his eye.

"What presence?" Delgorin breathed deeply through his nose and turned to head back to his cart.

"The wind dragon Quetzalcoatl, ruler of the skies, has landed for the first time in an age. Something significant must have happened while you were in the Temple of the Winds. Lady Quetzalcoatl does not often choose to make landfall, she forever soars in the skies." Vesth watched as the old man took the reigns from the other two horses and tied them to his cart.

"What Counsel would you give to me, old one? What action should I take?" Delgorin huffed.

"Your getting smarter, young soldier. I would suggest you go and find your charge and protect her. If Lady Quetzalcoatl is here for the reason I think she is, then Rielle will be in for a rough time. She must pass the test she is given, both mentally and physically." Vesth frowned.

"What kind of test?" Delgorin lifted the front of his cart and heaved it into motion.

"I cannot say. Lady Quetzalcoatl is normally light hearted, and as fickle as the breeze. However, she is unpredictable and if angered, her rage can rival that of all other Elemental Dragons. Lord Leviathan's anger, and Lord Tiamat's Impatience will pale in comparison to the force of Lady Quetzalcoatl's fury. Even if she is calling to Rielle, I would suggest you keep her away." Delgorin slipped past, his remaining horses in tow, and disappeared into the cities streets. Vesth growled and pulled on the horses' reigns.

"Come, we have work to do." The horses followed obediently and Vesth hurried back the way he had come, in search of Rielle.

He returned to where they had parted ways and followed the street Rielle had taken. It circled around and headed straight for the palace grounds. As Vesth grew near, he could smell something in the air, as if lightning had struck close by. He rushed ahead and found himself at the palace main gate where two guards stood staring towards the inner courtyard.

"What is going on?" He called as he got closer. Both guards ignored him and continued to stare. Vesth reached them and peered into the courtyard. At the center stood Rielle, facing a slender woman with flowing silver hair and billowing white clothes. Vesth frowned and nudged one of the guards out of his stupor.

"Who are you?" The guard asked, a little shaken. Vesth shoved the reigns of the horses into the guard's hands.

"Take these horses and stand outside the wall." The guard looked at his hand blankly and Vesth forcefully turned the other guard away.

"Do not look back into this courtyard until you receive orders to do otherwise."

"But we. . ." Vesth would have back-handed the man, but the horse jerked it's head and pulled the man off balance.

"Just do as I say. The business in the courtyard is only for the eyes of the High King and Ambassador Rielle." Vesth gave the guard a push and both men finally obeyed and made their way around to the other side of the gatehouse. Vesth slipped through the gate and scanned the courtyard. A few guards stood silently, watching with a dumbfounded expression on their faces. Vesth took this as a sign and kept his eyes averted from the two women who stood at the center of the courtyard.

Vesth worked his way quietly around until he reached the castle walls. He could see the High King, watching from just outside the castle doors. Vesth worried for a moment, and then realized that the High King did not have the same dumbfounded expression as the guards. Vesth carefully made his way to the High King's side.

"So Rielle did have someone with her when she arrived." The High King spoke without ever averting his gaze. Vesth nodded and turned, fixing his gaze on Rielle and ignoring the other woman entirely.

"Indeed your Highness. I am Vesth Dagda of Gentry. First Captain under Commander Thereon." The High King nodded.

"I have heard your name from King Yisu. You are a Dragon Blade?" Vesth nodded.

"Yes your Highness." The High King nodded once more.

"That is good. I believe I can trust you then. Make sure you protect my Cousin." Vesth watched the two women standing silently in the courtyard.

"With my life your Highness." The High King chuckled.

"I hope it will not come to that Captain. However, if you have information on the current situation, I would be most curious to hear it." Vesth frowned.

"I am not entirely sure, but if that person facing Rielle is who I fear it might be, I am not sure what the safest course of action would be. I am sorry your Highness." The High King shook his head.

"Do not be sorry captain. I am certain this is something that is beyond the understanding of simple soldiers such as us. But she feels much like someone I met a long time ago, when I was still very young." Vesth cast a sidelong glance at the High King. The High King noticed and understood the question in the look.

"Fafnir, Dragon guardian of Earth." Vesth felt a chill.

"Then it is as I fear. This must be Lady Quetzalcoatl, Dragon Guardian of Wind." The High King nodded with a frown.

"It does not surprise me. Though why she would show up here of all places eludes me." Vesth looked back to Rielle.

"I am afraid it may be our doing."

"Oh?" The High King looked curiously at Vesth. Vesth shook his head.

"I would rather not say, your Highness. I do not distrust you, but I would not wish to speak of such things out in the open where they could be overheard." The High King turned back to the courtyard.

"That may be wise." They stood silently, watching as the two women stared at one another. What seemed to Vesth to be an eternity passed before any words passed between them.

"Will you not speak young one?" The Silver haired woman's voice sighed and whispered like the wind, easily carrying to those who watched.

"What reason have I to speak, Lady Quetzalcoatl? It is you who called to me, and I have answered your call. It would be wrong of me to address you in too familiar a way." The Dragon smiled.

"You have spoken with my brothers have you not? Should I be so different?" Rielle nodded slightly.

"It is true that I have stood in the presence of both Lord Tiamat and Lord Leviathan, But I did not speak with them myself. I did not dare, it was Master Solidus who spoke, not I." The Dragon nodded.

"I see. I do not blame you of course, Both my brothers were quite angry with Master Solidus when you met them." Rielle thought for a moment.

"I did have a question, If you do not mind my asking milady." The Dragon nodded.

"You may ask." Rielle thought for a moment more, looking for words to voice her question.

"I have noticed in my travels that even among the great Dragons, Master Solidus is referred to as 'Master'."

"Indeed." The Dragon replied, waiting for the question.

"Why is that? To my knowledge the only ones left on this world older than Master Solidus would be the dark creatures in the Mercury Mountains and the four Guardian Dragons. I have not seen, nor heard of, any one in any society who has ever called their juniors Master." The Dragon nodded several times.

"Yes indeed. I understand why you would question this. But there are several reasons why you would not quite understand. First, we come from a time long past, the Age of Creation. In those times, any who could achieve a certain level of expertise or power were called Master, including mortals. Second, the Balance Mages have always been held in high regard and given the title Master. But this is an age without magic, and the Balance Mages are all but extinct. You should still understand this to a degree however, since you have spent time in the presence of Master Solidus." Rielle nodded, but waited quietly, anticipating more words from the Dragon. The Dragon nodded in return and continued.

"Third, Master Solidus himself is a bit of a special case. He sees what others cannot. He changes what others cannot. And he exists where others cannot. Beyond that his power is nearly absolute so long as he remains within the balance. He easily rivals the power of we four Dragon Guardians." Vesth felt a shock travel through him, and beside him he noticed that the High King's sword arm twitched. Rielle opened her mouth to speak again but the Dragon raised her hand.

"That is enough. I have already spoken more than I should, and we have other business to attend to." Rielle half bowed.

"Of course, Lady Quetzalcoatl, I nearly forgot myself. Why is it that you have called me here?" Vesth stepped forward and dropped to one knee.

"Please hold a moment." Rielle noticed him, seemingly for the first time. The Dragon glanced over her shoulder and peered at Vesth with milk white eyes. Vesth felt his mind begin to fog and quickly bowed his head.

"Please, if it is not too much of a bother to you Great Dragon, may I please request that we be given a chance to clear all bystanders from the courtyard before you speak?" Vesth waited nervously, unsure if he had addressed the woman correctly.

"For what purpose, mortal?" Vesth cleared his throat carefully.

"If what you have to discuss with Miss Rielle has to do with recent events, I would not be comfortable with there being this many witnesses. The High King beside me here I would trust as Master Solidus has already spoken with him previously, but the guards and any servants here could easily gossip or be coerced by the enemy to hear what transpires here. As we are under the direction of Master Solidus and he has instructed us to be cautious, I do not wish to take any risks that could jeopardize his plans." Again Vesth sat still, nervously waiting a reply.

"And you think it would be best to remove them?" Vesth nodded.

"I do, Mistress." Vesth felt the High King step up beside him.

"Please, Milady, between myself and the young soldier here we can clear the courtyard in just a few moments. I do wish to think that my city is safe, but even during Master Solidus's last visit we were beset by a demon and Rielle was forced to remove the creature. I would not wish for your magnificence to be placed at an inconvenience because a creature from the chaos convinced itself to attack or take from you in some way." The Dragon was quiet for a few moments and then she nodded.

"Very well, but be quick." The High King nodded and tapped Vesth on the shoulder.

"Let's go Captain." Vesth stood and he and the High King moved quickly about the courtyard gathering the few people standing in the open and leading them by hand through the doors to the castle. Once they were finished the High King entered the castle and closed the door behind him, leaving Vesth to stand guard.

"All is ready, Milady." Vesth called, bending at the waist in a shallow bow. The Dragon did not acknowledge Vesth but instead turned back to Rielle.

"The reason I called you here was your recent contact with Lady Sidhe." Rielle nodded.

"I see. I did speak with Soaring Zephyr Sidhe a short time ago. I did so under the instruction of Master Solidus." The Dragon nodded.

"So you did. I have called you here to see if you are worthy, and have the strength necessary, to make use of Lady Sidhe's gift." Vesth frowned deeply. Rielle nodded slowly.

"If you speak of The Cloak of Sidhe, then I can assure you that I have already made use of the power that Soaring Zephyr Sidhe granted me in return for cleansing her temple." The Dragon shook her head.

"As Elemental Dragon of the Wind, I will not simply allow a mortal to carry something as powerful as a Cloak without my approval." Now Rielle also frowned.

"Again, Lady Quetzalcoatl, I am working under the direction of Grandmaster Silver Mage Solidus. Should you stand in my way I will do whatever I must to complete the task given me." The Dragon burst into laughter. A light silvery sound that would have been beautiful were it not terrifying.

"And you, a mortal, presume you have the power to contend with me? Mistress of the Storms and second only to Soaring Zephyr Sidhe?" The laughter cut short, replaced by a stare colder than a savage blizzard. "Utter Heresy."

Rielle carefully removed the curved sword from her side and sat it on the ground next to her, then she pulled the cloth tube from her back and began to untie it.

"But miss Rielle." Vesth protested.

"Be silent Vesth." Rielle's tone gave no room for disobedience and Vesth bowed his head. The cloth fell to the ground and Rielle held the Patriarch before her, ready to draw the blade from it's scabbard. The Dragon's expression didn't change.

"You think you can wield that blade?" Rielle's features hardened and her gaze was nearly as cold as the Dragon's.

"I will do what must be done, there is no option to fail." Thunder played across the sky as the clouds above them darkened. The wind picked up and swirled around the courtyard and a pale white aura seemed to settle around Rielle. From that point Vesth could no longer follow what was happening.

Voices filled his mind, all speaking at once, and none of them making sense. When the voices finally faded away, and his mind was no longer overwhelmed with chaos, everything was over. Rielle was slipping the Patriarch back into his scabbard and the Dragon Quetzalcoatl stood close by, her expression no longer cold and angry.

"If you learn to move, even if only a few steps, to loosen your body before you evoke the Cloak of Sidhe you will find that your movements will be faster and easier to control. Rielle nodded and began to slide the Patriarch back into the cloth tube.

"Thank you, Lady Quetzalcoatl. I will remember your council." The Dragon nodded and finally turned to look back at Vesth. Vesth lowered his eyes and waited for her to speak.

"Be sure you protect her, Broken One. She is special." Vesth bowed.

"My only intention has ever been to protect Miss Rielle. That is not going to change, regardless of the circumstances or whether or not she is considered special." The Dragon nodded.

"That is good. If ever I return to the earth, I will hold you responsible if she is put off in any way." Vesth, still bowed, placed his fist over his heart.

"As you will, Milady." The Dragon nodded once more, and waved once to Rielle, before disappearing altogether. Vesth took a few breaths to calm his beating heart, then stood and made his way to help Rielle as she began to sway from exhaustion.

Chapter Sixteen

"My cousin's skill with a blade as grown at an impressive rate." The High King sat at the head of a long table set with enough food for a feast. Vesth sat to the king's right, eating from what he had been given.

"I would agree, Your Highness. I have never known anyone who learned as quickly as Miss Rielle." The High King nodded a few times, chewing his food carefully before speaking.

"I would think that her teacher is partially responsible for the speed at which she has grown." Vesth shook his head.

"I am no great teacher, your Highness. I can only show miss Rielle the motions, she is the one who has taught herself how to use them." The High King chuckled.

"I think you sell yourself short Captain. You are a Dragon Blade after all. That is no mean feat for one as young as you. But I suppose you are entitled to believe what you wish." Vesth shrugged.

"I am a simple Soldier, your Highness. I can only act

according to my duty." The High King also shrugged and drank from his wine glass.

"What will you be doing now?" He asked, changing the subject. Vesth sat his utensils aside and looked across the table at the King.

"We planned on traveling to the Temple of Water, Your Highness. It is the next temple we must visit, according to Master Solidus." The High King slowly lowered his glass and carefully eyed Vesth.

"So you plan on traveling the Pilgrim's Road?" Vesth turned his head slightly, clearly not understanding. The High King stood silently, motioning for Vesth to follow. They moved quickly through the castle, startled servants scrambling out of the way. They entered the castle's library and the High King ordered the librarians to leave, locking the doors behind them. He continued through the forest of shelves and books until they found themselves at the back of the library. The High King turned, a serious expression on his face.

"What you see here you will not speak of to anyone." He was not asking. Vesth nodded, tension growing in his gut. The High King turned back to the shelves and pulled out several books before reaching out and twisting a candlestick attached to a shelf on a nearby wall. There was the sound of clicking mechanisms and then a groan as the shelf slowly slid forward, revealing a space behind it. The High king entered the space and Vesth followed close behind, traveling down a narrow passage.

Vesth heard the bookshelf behind them sliding back into place. It was difficult to walk down the dark passage and Vesth found himself holding onto the wall to guide him. After a few moments a light flared into existence before him as the High King lit a candle and they entered a small room. The High King went about the room lighting candles and Vesth noted that the room seemed like a war pavilion.

There were a few shelves with books and a desk in one corner, but the room itself was dominated by a large table in the center that was laid out with a map of Galbrea. The High King extinguished his candle and sat it on the desk and motioned for Vesth to stand near the table.

"When I was young I enjoyed wandering the castle, exploring each corner looking for secrets I could call my own. It took me ages to figure out how to open this passage, but when I did I was rewarded with discovering this room." Vesth examined the table and shelves and noticed that they were covered in arcane symbols. Symbols he had only ever seen in one place before. He shuddered with the memories and looked back at the High King, one hand subconsciously covering his stomach.

"What is this place?" The High King reached down and opened a book set in a notch in the table. Immediately lights covered the table, showing armies and their movements.

"This is a place that was sealed away to avoid destruction during the Purge. It takes the words of the book in the slot and projects them on the map of Galbrea. Allowing you to see the words as they take place. This book is from before the Age of Peace. It details the positions and movements of the different factions that were fighting at the time. With this table you can see those movements and the battles that take place." The High King closed the book and the lights disappeared. He removed the book and placed it back on a shelf.

He looked through the other books, his finger hovering

over each one until it paused over the one he sought. He took it down and placed it on the table and opened it. Lights covered the table once again, four points connected by lines spanning across the entire continent. The High King placed his finger on the first point.

"This is the Pilgrim's Road. A road traveled by those trying to attain enlightenment. You have already visited the Temple of Wind." He slid his finger across the map, following the line until it reached the next point in the far east of Laytrow.

"And now you are trying to get to the Temple of Water." Vesth nodded, not sure where the discussion was going. The High King turned the next page of the book and the points turned red and unclear shapes began to form around each one.

"Each Temple was once protected by a Guardian that had to be convinced of the Pilgrim's good intentions before they were allowed to enter the Temple itself." Vesth frowned.

"There was no Guardian at the Temple of Wind. Will the other Temples still have their Guardians?" The High King turned another page of the book and now the Capitals of Hortaal, Laytrow, and Gentry also lit up, and a small point in the southern part of the Serpent Tongue mountians.

"Eventually the guardians began to die out and the way to the Temples were entrusted to the rulers of each of the newly formed countries at the end of the Age of War." Vesth looked at the High King, who nodded to his unasked question.

"Yes, I am the current guardian of the Temple of Wind. However, The way to the Temple was opened to you by Master Solidus and so you did not need to seek me out to find your way. However, the other Temples are sealed. As the main chamber of the Temple of Wind was hidden, so are the other Temples hidden from intrusion. If you want to get into the Temple of Water you will first have to travel to Yal' Tora and speak with Knight King Kartor Del Cresol." Vesth's frown deepened.

"The Knight King is unwelcoming to strangers. I doubt he would help us so easily." The High King nodded.

"He knows my cousin Rielle well enough, as I have sent her to treat with him before. He should be willing to see you and listen to what you have to say. Whether or not he will help is going to be up to you. You must convince him that the reason you seek the Temple is a righteous one and that you are worthy of entering." Vesth nodded.

"I see. I am sure that Miss Rielle will be able to make a convincing argument." Vesth felt the tension within him return as the High King shook his head.

"He will see you, but as a knight he does not see women as legitimate speakers in his court. He listens to Rielle only because she is of Royal blood and an official ambassador of Hortaal who speaks directly for me. Since she will not be on official business for Hortaal, Kartor will see no reason to let her speak in his court. However," The High King looked at Vesth who did not like the direction things were going.

"You, Vesth Dagda, are a Dragon Blade. In the Knight King's eyes you have proven yourself in battle and are worthy of speaking in his court." Vesth frowned.

"I have never understood the need to fight for personal honor. Fighting does not prove one's personal worth."

"To the Laytrow Plainsmen, it does." The High King argued. "Prove to the Laytrow court that you are worthy, and the Knight King will likely give you the secret to finding the Temple of Water." Vesth grumbled, but reluctantly nodded.

"I understand, your Highness." The High King nodded.

"Very good. The Guardian of the Temple of Earth is King Yisu, I do not imagine he will be too hard to convince. Both Rielle and Yourself are already held in high esteem by his court. But, as such, I do not know who the Guardian of the Temple of Fire is. I do not believe the High Priest Borsa would be given knowledge of such a place." Vesth looked at the table examining each point, picturing each place in his mind. His eyes fell on the last point, in the Serpent Tongue Mountains, and he shuddered.

"I believe I know who was."

"Tiamat, Dragon Guardian of Fire." Came a voice from the passageway behind them. Both men turned like lightning, swords drawn.

"No need for that now." Solidus stepped from the shadows cast by the flickering candlelight, hands raised. The High King relaxed and Vesth half bowed.

"So my hunch was correct." Vesth stated as he returned his sword to it's scabbard. Solidus nodded.

"As you know, Borsa could not be trusted with something such as the Temple of Fire. In the end we decided it was best if the secrets were left in Tiamat's care." The High King also returned his sword to it's place at his side and examined the map on the table again.

"Is it wise to intrude on Lord Tiamat's Solitude?" Solidus chuckled.

"Tiamat is an irritable old curmudgeon, but he knows his duty. By the time Rielle must face him, she will have the strength to prove her worthiness and command his respect." The High King nodded slowly.

"Then there is nothing left for me to do but pray to the Six for her success." Solidus nodded, and then removed a small bundle from his cloak and held it out to Vesth.

"You will need this for your trials to come. Keep it with you at all times, you will know when to use it." Vesth reached out and took the bundle warily. It was light and soft, but somehow it felt as if it were as strong as steel.

"You will need to leave immediately for Yal' Tora. Rielle has awakened and already left." Vesth's eyes grew wide and he rushed to leave, but Solidus reached out and barred his path.

"Do not search for her. She is already beyond your reach. She is drawn to the Temple of Water, the only way you will catch her again is to travel to Yal' Tora and speak with the Knight King." Vesth scowled, but nodded as he saw lightning flash in Solidus's eyes. Solidus nodded and allowed him to pass.

"Now," He turned to the High King. "There is a part for you to play, Morien Toriel, and it will take much preparation if you are to be ready." Solidus waved one hand through the air and the pages of the book on the table turned rapidly. As the images on the table changed the High King's eyes widened in surprise and Solidus nodded solemnly.

"Let it begin."

* * *

Nysisset frowned deeply at the old man standing in front of them. He held the reigns of two horses out to them, grinning all the while.

"I see your companion is doing well." Delgorin told Segine as the knight accepted the reigns. Segine cleared his throat uncomfortably.

"She has been in ill humors most of the day." Delgorin chuckled and Nysisset's frown deepened further.

"I was hoping that Lord Leviathan had drowned you." She grumbled. Delgorin placed one hand over his heart, pretending to be hurt.

"Come now miss Nysisset, there is no need for such hostility." The old man looked at the sky, shading his eyes from the sun.

"The Darkmoon Cycle has already passed, you should feel much better by now." Nysisset hissed quietly and pulled her cloak more tightly around her shoulders. Delgorin chuckled for a moment and then sighed.

"How did you know where to find us Master Delgorin?" Segine asked, hoping to shift the old man's attention away from Nysisset. Delgorin's expression sobered.

"Master Solidus sent me here to give you instructions." Nysisset grumbled. Delgorin stared her down.

"This is important, Darkling, Lady Quetzalcoatl made landfall in Terramine." Nysisset's eyes widened in surprise. Delgorin nodded.

"Things in the city are not entirely stable, and since it is still only a few days past the Darkmoon Cycle you should do your best to contain your power and the amulet you carry. Master Solidus said that the powers of Darkness have not been felt in most of Galbrea for well over a thousand years. With the elements shifting within the city to settle after Lady Quetzalcoatl visited, it might not take much to disturb the balance there." Nysisset nodded in dejected understanding.

"Why would Lady Quetzalcoatl choose to make landfall in

the city?" Delgorin patted Segine's charger and it bobbed it's head in approval.

"She wished to meet with Miss Rielle." Segine felt a jolt in his gut.

"So Miss Rielle and Vesth are in Terramine?" His stomach fell again as Delgorin shook his head.

"They left four days ago, I was not told to where. But Master Solidus instructed that you speak with High King Morien in Terramine. You are not meant to rejoin them just yet, there is a part for you to play."

"What part?" Segine asked. Delgorin shrugged.

"I don't know. Master Solidus only instructed me to tell you to speak with the High King." Nysisset watched the old man as he spoke.

"Why the sudden change? You speak of Master Solidus with a more reverent tone than you did before." Delgorin locked eyes with Nysisset and she felt a ping of nervousness as she saw the power hidden behind the old man's eyes.

"As Solidus watches over the balance in the world he is simply our elder brother and peer, the first of the Alenon Mages. But in times such as these, when he takes an active role in directing the balance he is no longer Silver Mage Solidus. When he drops his act of lightheartedness and simplicity, he becomes Grandmaster Balance Mage Pravin Solidus. His words carry the same command as the voices of the Six. Something stirs and Master Solidus is the only one who can direct us to protect the balance. I no longer follow the wishes of my brother, I obey the command of my Master." The air around them felt heavy and thick as Delgorin remained silent for a few more moments before glancing at Segine.

"Remember, speak with the High King, He can direct you further." With this said, the old man simply vanished. The horses danced nervously and Segine patted them reassuringly. They stood quietly for several minutes before Nysisset shook herself.

"Come, we ride for Terramine." With new found strength she lifted herself into her saddle and took the reigns from Segine.

"If we ride hard we can be there in two days time." Segine nodded solemnly and mounted his charger, turning it and leading the way through the forest.

* * *

Vesth cursed himself under his breath for what seemed the hundredth time. Several people in the street heard and gave him a wide berth. He rode quickly toward the Knight King's palace, his horse snorting at anyone who didn't step aside quickly enough.

The guards at the palace gates called him to halt and then allowed him to pass when he stated his name. He left his horse with a stable hand and walked briskly into the palace where he was lead by a servant to the court. He waited impatiently for several minutes while other business was discussed before his presence was announced. He was ushered inside and the door closed behind him.

"Captain Vesth Dagda of the First Gentry Legion." Vesth noticed that it was not the Knight King who addressed him, but a large knight to his left.

"It is the understanding of this court that you have come to make a personal inquiry of the Knight King." Vesth bowed at the waist.

"That is correct." Vesth noticed that most of the knight's in the room were watching him with something akin to annoyance.

"What makes you think yourself worthy of addressing this court?" Vesth did his best not to frown.

"As previously mentioned I am a Captain of the First Legion under Commander Thereon. As such I am well versed in strategy both on land and at sea. I have proven my prowess in battle and have been recognized by King Yisu for my skill. I also come bearing the approval of High King Morien Toriel of Hortaal. It is also the High King who directed me to seek out this court and pose my inquiry to the Knight King." Several knights nodded their approval, the others simply continued to watch passively.

"What is your inquiry?" Vesth eyed each of the knight's in the room.

"I would ask that only the most senior and trusted knights of the court be allowed to hear my inquiry. The matter is of utmost import, not only to Hortaal and Gentry, but Laytrow as well. I would not wish any sensitive information to leave without the direct approval of the Knight King himself." The knight to the right of the Knight King stood angrily.

"You have no right to speak in such a disrespectful manner in this court." Vesth locked eyes with the knight.

"I spoke with no such disrespect. I spoke with regards to the court and safety of the kingdom in mind. I am not saying that any of the knights in this room are untrustworthy, But accidents can happen and information that is supposed to remain private has a higher chance of escaping to unwanted ears the greater the number that hears it. This would put many lives in danger including my own and maybe even some of those who are present. This is a risk I will not take." The knight to the left of the Knight King spoke once again.

"We did receive a missive from High King Morien regarding this matter. He is also convinced it is of the utmost importance. What is the subject of this inquiry, and who sent you to gain answers here?" Vesth was growing weary of the constant court manners he was told to maintain.

"I was sent in regards to a certain Temple said to be protected by the Knight King." A few of the knights exchanged glances.

"Who sent you here?" Vesth eyed each of the knight's watching their expressions.

"High King Morien Toriel and Master Solidus, the Hermit Mage." The knights all shifted uncomfortably at the mention of a mage, but it was obvious to Vesth that most of them did not recognize Master Solidus's name.

"I object to this claim!" Shouted one knight at the far end of the bar.

"General Proteus, why do you object?" Vesth recognized the man's name as one of the Generals in charge of the Great South-Western Gate.

"This, Solidus, is not to be trusted. He was personally responsible for the destruction of the South-Western Gate. And according to reports he also destroyed the Northern Gate where, also according to reports, He died." Many of the knights in the room mumbled amongst each other.

"I was stationed at the Great Northern Gate. I assure you that Master Solidus is not dead." Vesth spoke before anyone else could agree with the General's objection.

"And though it is true that the Great Gates were destroyed, it was for good reason. I doubt there is a man in this room who did not witness the Blood Moon Cycle. Our losses would have been catastrophic during the Blood Moon had Master Solidus not destroyed both Gates." Many of the knights muttered agreement.

"I do not believe the Gates destruction was warranted. Whatever might have come through the Gates on that night, our forces were great enough to handle with ease."

"The Blood Moon Cycle would have rendered even the most skilled fighters weak. Even the slightest scratch or injury would have been enough to kill. It is the way of the world since it was created." The General shook his head.

"I have seen no evidence to support that superstitious nonsense." Vesth was about to call the man a fool before something surfaced in his memory.

"Perhaps you only wish to stop my progress because you were shamed in front of your troops by Master Solidus." The General sputtered and Vesth knew he was correct.

"I heard from Ambassador Rielle Toriel Lyvinius that you would not heed Master Solidus's warnings and he had to save you from a demon host." The General slammed his fist on the bar, clearly outraged.

"No such thing happened! How dare you slander my name in this court." Vesth was done playing with this man and his eyes grew cold.

"If you try to stand in my way it will be my blade that shames you." All eyes turned to the General. The man's face was red with anger.

"If you want your death to come so young, then I will meet you on the field of battle." Vesth nodded, undeterred.

"Think carefully before you accept this duel Captain." Cautioned the knight to the left of the Knight King. "General Proteus is a seasoned veteran and a Dragon Blade." Vesth nodded once again.

"As am I. I will not let this man bar my path for petty Pride." Many of the knights looked at Vesth in disbelief. Then, after remaining silent throughout the exchange, the Knight King stood.

"This matter will be settled on the dueling field at sundown. All in the court are required to attend." The Knight King's deep voice reverberated through the halls and each knight stood in turn and bowed to the Knight King before exiting. Last to leave was the Knight King himself. He paused and ran a careful eye over Vesth. Then, turning to leave, he said,

"Win this duel, and we will discuss the Temple of Water."

* * *

Vesth stood silently on the packed dirt of the arena floor, his hand resting at the ready on his sword. General Proteus entered from the other end of the arena wearing light dueling armor. The mood in the arena itself was solemn. The knights in attendance sat quietly watching the two combatants prepare for battle. The Knight King and his two advisers sat in a booth separated from the other knights.

"Are you ready to lose?" The General asked. Vesth's hardened glare landed heavily on the man across from him.

"You are a fool to bar my path. If you are so blinded by your pride that you cannot see the danger that we are all in, then I will not hesitate to strike you down." General Proteus harrumphed.

"You're a cocky young brat. You will not live to regret crossing me." One of the Knight King's advisers stood.

"Combatants face the Knight King." Vesth and General Proteus turned and faced the Knight King and bowed deeply at the waist.

"Combatants turn and salute." Both men turned and drew their swords, placing them across their chest in salute.

"Combatants begin." The General rushed Vesth with surprising speed that reminded Vesth of Segine. The General aimed his strike for Vesth's head, intent on cleaving him in two. Vesth sidestepped him and deflected a second attack. Vesth noted that General Proteus was not as fast as Segine, but his blows were much heavier. The two men traded blows for a moment and then backed off.

Vesth let his sword point dip low to the ground and kept his grip loose. The General kept his two-handed sword raised, turning the blade so that Vesth could see the rearing dragon at the base of the blade.

"A picture on a sword does not impress me." Vesth stated coldly, twisting his blade to reveal his own dragon. "I am not a knight, I do not care for personal honor. You cannot intimidate me by parading your achievements in front of me. I do not care, and my patience for dealing with your stupidity wears thin." The General's face flushed red with anger.

"You, Whelp, will eat your words." The General rushed Vesth again, this time twisting mid-strike. Vesth caught the General's blade with his own, sliding it away from his body at an angle. The General recovered quickly and committed himself to a heavy-handed onslaught. Vesth found each successive blow more and more difficult to meet head on and was eventually forced to deflect each attack and retreat.

The General, taking this as a sign of weakness, pushed harder to drive Vesth into the wall where he could not retreat. Vesth immediately realized that the General had given into his blood lust and would not stop until he had managed to land a fatal blow. Vesth's eyes followed his enemy's blade as it made concentric circles and arcs. It was very similar to Segine's style of fighting, though more fluid and tighter in practice.

Vesth could see the wall behind him coming in quickly and threw as much force as he could at a right angle to the General's blade. The General continued to push, but Vesth had managed to slow the attack enough to slip around the General and roll to gain some distance. When Vesth returned to his feet he took his sword in both hands for the first time in the fight and raised it carefully above his head, the point aiming at the sky behind him.

"I see now. You fight in a fashion similar to a knight I know." The General grumbled under his breath.

"Having seen my style of fighting before will not save you. You lack the strength and commitment to the fight to beat me." Vesth frowned deeply and strength flooded his body as he slowly opened his first gate, focusing on the 'key' in the pouch at his side.

"Don't act like you are superior. I fight for something other than myself, and someone who fights for others will always have strength over those who fight selfishly. Even if I was not strong enough to beat you, it takes more than physical strength to win a battle." The General snorted and raised his sword, ready to attack again.

"What would a snot nosed kid like you know about battle?" Now Vesth growled, low and menacing.

"You may fight in tournaments, but I am willing to wager that I have seen more true combat than you. The sea is far more treacherous and unforgiving than the land. You look down on everyone, thinking you are better than they." Vesth bent his knees slightly and leaned forward into his stance, twisting until he was watching the General through a narrow space between his arm and sword blade.

"It is time you were toppled from your high horse." The General lowered the tip of his sword and rushed Vesth, aiming to run him through.

"You Are Not Better Than Me!" Vesth waited until the last moment, then spun his blade with both hands, knocking the General's sword off course. Continuing to spin the blade, Vesth turned and stepped forward, faster than the General could react, and drove the point of his blade through the General's left shoulder. He quickly removed the blade, twisted behind the General, and hamstrung the man. Vesth slid to a stop, spraying dust into the air and flicking the blood from his sword as General Proteus fell to the ground.

"Unfortunately for you, I am better." Vesth stated. General Proteus rolled onto his back and threw his sword as best as he could with his good arm. Vesth was ready and spun around, striking the sword out of the air, and driving the point into the hard ground. Vesth calmly walked over and stood over his crippled opponent. The General's face was beet red with embarrassment and pain, but most of all, rage.

"Finish me then. Or are you just going to stand there like a spineless coward?" Vesth reversed his grip on his sword and drove the blade into the General's right shoulder, piercing his dueling armor like paper. The General growled like a hurt animal and Vesth dropped to one knee and spoke quietly.

"Only a coward seeks death as a way to escape his shame. I will not let you get away so easily. I have taken from you what you prized so highly. Never again will you fight with the same strength you did before. You will live, constantly reminded of your folly, and now everyone here knows you for what you are." Vesth stood, removed his sword from the General, wiped it clean, and returned it to it's scabbard. The Knight King stood from his seat.

"The duel ends in favor of Captain Vesth Dagda. General Proteus well be taken to receive medical care and then be officially removed from his seat on the council. A special council of five will be held tonight after the evening meal to discuss his replacement and the request of the Captain. The rest of you are dismissed to attend to your other duties." The knights in the arena stood and bowed to the Knight King and then went their separate ways. Many of the knights saluted Vesth as they left and he did his best to politely return the gesture. Several servants entered the arena with a stretcher and made their way to the General's side.

"Get your hands off of me!" Proteus snapped angrily. "I will make sure you pay for this day, Whelp. Don't think you have beaten me." The man did his best to lash out at the servants who were trying to load him onto the stretcher, and managed to fight them off for several moments until a heavy gauntlet struck him in the jaw, knocking him unconscious. Vesth turned in surprise to see one of the Knight King's advisers directing the servants to take the general away, adjusting his gauntlet after punching the man.

"You fought well." The knight stated, placing his fist over his chest in salute.

"You are quite skilled for one of your age." Vesth returned the salute, though he did not smile.

"This was an unnecessary waste of time. There are important things I must attend to and this delay wears on my nerves." The knight nodded.

"I understand you are eager to be on your way, I have been made aware of what is going on outside the city. Strange creatures roam the land, attacking unwary travelers. Dark figures lurk among the people, and rumors are beginning to circulate that Tyr' Anon has been abandoned." Vesth frowned deeply.

"It was not abandoned. It was destroyed, by the High Priest himself." The knight also frowned.

"Borsa seems to have much to answer for. I think it would be wise for you to join myself and the Knight King for a meal. There are things we do not know that you may be able to share with us. We have received a letter from High King Morien Toriel instructing us to gather our forces and prepare them for battle, but we were given no reason why." Vesth nodded.

"I will tell you what I know, But I do not know why the High King would call for an army to be assembled. He is likely acting under the direction of Master Solidus. I was given my own task to fulfill and was not told what others would be doing."

"We also received word from a man who referred to himself only as Brother Aegis." Vesth eyes widened. The knight continued.

"He suggested we be wary of the one named Solidus, but that it would be wise to follow his council for the time being." Vesth nodded.

"Brother Aegis leads an organization who's goal it is to try and maintain the balance of the world's power. They fight any magic users or others who attempt to use their power for personal gain or destruction. He is wise and a good person to look to for council if it is necessary." The Knight nodded.

"Very well. This Brother Aegis also asked us to inform you that two of your companions are with him now, under the instruction of High King Morien." Vesth felt relief wash over him.

"That is good. We worried that they had been lost." The Knight nodded.

"They are well, and will be working with Brother Aegis for a short while. But I think it would now be wise to join the Knight King and discuss the current situation." Vesth nodded and motioned for the Knight to lead the way and followed him out of the arena and towards the palace.

Epilogue

Vesth rode quietly through the main city gates. The early morning sun filling the plains with golden light as Vesth carefully recited the Knight King's instructions to himself over again so as not to forget. A few minutes passed after leaving the city before Vesth sensed the presence following him, dark and tainted.

One hand rested carefully on his sword handle, the other pulled slightly on the reigns to slow his horse. A few more minutes passed and he could hear horses hooves striking the hard road behind him. They got closer and closer and then matched his pace when they reached him. Vesth's grip tightened on his sword.

"That won't be necessary, Captain." The voice was dry, but not threatening. Vesth did not loosen his grip.

"What is your business with me?" A humorless chuckle answered him.

"I am here to help you. I can lead you to where you wish to go." Vesth glanced over his shoulder to look at the man following him. He stayed several paces behind Vesth, his face obscured by a deep, sand colored hood.

"And what would you know of what I seek?" The man nodded beneath his hood.

"I know you seek the Temple of Water, and the one Rielle Toriel Lyvinius. I can lead you to both." Vesth scowled, not pleased by how much the man seemed to know.

"Why would you help? What is it you want in return?" The man was quiet for a moment before answering.

"I do not want anything in return, as your goals coincide with my own. As for why..." The man looked off towards the Serpent's Tongue mountains. "My previous employer did not conduct himself well, and I feel it necessary to join the battle taking place here." The man had previously spoken without emotion, but Vesth noticed the slightest hint of passion in what the man said. They continued on silently for several minutes before Vesth spoke again.

"I would know your name."

"You may call me Keliter." Was the reply.

"Where can I find Rielle?" Vesth could almost feel the man grinning behind him.

"In two day's time she will be in a town North of here. She will make it to the Temple of Water within the week." Vesth nodded and nudged his horse into a trot.

"Then we ride North." The horse behind him matched his pace and Vesth's stomach knotted as he heard the quiet reply.

"Hopefully we find her in time."

The End

To be Continued in Book 3: End of Cycles